UNWRITTEN LAW

STEELE BROTHERS BOOK ONE

EDEN FINLEY

Paperback Edition

Unwritten Law Copyright © 2018 by Eden Finley

Cover Illustration Copyright © AngstyG
http://www.angstyg.com

Beta read by Leslie Copeland
https://www.lescourtauthorservices.com/
Email: lcopelandwrites@gmail.com

Copy-edited by Xterraweb Edits
http://editing.xterraweb.com/

All rights reserved.
This book or any portion thereof may not be reproduced or used in any manner whatsoever without the express written permission of the publisher.
For information regarding permission, write to:
Eden Finley - permissions - edenfinley@gmail.com

DISCLAIMER/TRIGGER WARNINGS

This is a story about mistaken identity—a physical relationship built on lies and deception.

While Eden Finley aims to write light-hearted escapes, and this book is mainly uplifting with a crazy premise, it does deal with some serious issues such as domestic abuse. These scenes are in no way explicit, but you might want to reconsider if you have triggers.

Names, characters, businesses, places, events and incidents are either the products of the author's imagination or used in a fictitious manner.

1
LAWSON

*R*ejection sucks, but there's something fundamentally interesting about the fragile male ego. Breaking up with people has become routine for me. So much so I can almost predict the words they're going to say before I've even ended it.

Take this guy for instance. Being in a crowded restaurant won't stop him from flipping his lid when I tell him we're done. Public is best for a breakup, but that doesn't mean it can't backfire. I'm tempted to blow the tealight candles out. Not only because it makes the mood too romantic but because there's a real risk of catching fire if he starts throwing things.

Paranoid, maybe, but it wouldn't be the first time.

I examine the guy across from me, trying to figure him out. He's young—still a teenager. Really pretty face, big blue eyes, pouty lips, and luscious dark hair any woman would be jealous of.

When it comes to picking the right words to let him

down gently, it's going to be hard. When hot, young play toys hear *I'm just not that into you*, it gets ugly.

This one is the type who doesn't like to be broken up with. His actual feelings don't come into play. Fooling around for a month is not a promise of forever, and I guarantee he understands this. He's just going to be pissed he didn't break it off first. He won't grovel, promise to do better, or try to hold onto whatever he thinks he has with me. No, this is going to be a shit show.

He reaches for my hand on top of the table, but I reach for my glass of water instead and take a sip. We haven't ordered food yet, and when the waitress comes by to ask if we're ready, I send her away and tell her to give us a few minutes.

My date's brows pinch together. "What's wrong?"

"I don't think this is working. You're a great guy, and we've had fun, but you're eighteen years old. You should be going out with guys your own age."

"You're only twenty-three. That's barely an age gap."

I almost choke. "Uh, I may've understated my age a little." Or a lot.

"How old are you?"

"That doesn't matter. We're not suited. I want things you can't give me."

"I don't see the problem if we're still having fun."

"Right. Uh, the thing is, I want to settle down, and I can't do that with an eighteen-year-old."

"Wait. You're really breaking up with me?" His voice gets high-pitched.

Oooh boy, I know the signs. If I don't defuse this, I could

very well be getting slapped in a minute. It's happened before. "It's not you, it's m—"

"Don't even try to pull that bullshit line with me."

"I'm sorry."

In three ... two ... I fuse my eyes shut. And there it is—not a slap, but a glass of water dumped on my head. My predictions aren't science, but they're damn near close to it.

"You can fuck off, Anders." He storms out, the sway of his hips accentuating his diva-like exit.

"You too, Kade ..." Or is it Kale? Eh, can't remember.

I grab the napkin off the table and wipe my face and shirt. All in all, not an overly bad breakup. There's been worse.

Taking my phone from my pocket, I send a message to my brother.

You owe me, asshole. Coast is clear.

Not thirty seconds later, the real Anders sits in the seat across from me, and I don't have to say a word.

"Law, don't start. I'm buying you dinner to make up for it."

"Are you also going to give me your shirt?" I nod at his nice, dry, blue T-shirt.

"Uh, no."

"And seriously? You told him you were twenty-three?"

"We could totally pass for twenty-three."

"You have to stop with the hyperactive twinks, man. They're getting too much."

Anders winces. "Straight dudes aren't allowed to say twinks."

"Sure, we are. And thanks to doing your dirty work, I'm gay by association, so I'm definitely allowed to say it. This has to be the last time. I can't keep breaking up with guys for you."

My brother is the most confident guy you'd ever meet, except when it comes to conflict. He can flirt with anyone—which he shamelessly does—and get up in front of a room full of hundreds of people without breaking a sweat. But one-on-one, talking about the real stuff, he turns into a bumbling, shaky leaf. Using me to avoid dealing with it isn't the answer, and I know I'm making it worse by playing along, but I don't have much of a choice in the matter. I don't want to cut him off and cause a setback.

Anders hangs his head and speaks low. "It's easier this way."

"Have you thought about going back to counselling—"

"Lawson …"

"Anderson," I mimic back. "I'm done. How would you deal with this if you didn't have a twin brother? I'm enabling you. I need to stand my ground this time." *Sure, because this is so different than the last time I gave him this speech.*

"You been bitching to Mum again?"

"No."

"Okay, fine. No more breakups. I'll go back to being celibate."

I laugh. "Think you'd be able to after becoming accustomed to having a new guy warm your bed every month?"

"What about you? You haven't been on a date in forever."

"How did we start talking about me? You're the one with issues."

Anders scoffs. "Keep telling yourself that, brother. We both know when it comes to love we're both fucked."

He has a point. Women don't seem to keep my interest longer than a few months anymore. That, and they have a hard time dealing with my relationship with Anders. They don't understand what it's like to have a twin who needs them. I've had a lot of girlfriends, but none I'd consider a serious relationship. I've never had visions of marriage and kids with any of them.

"How about we forget about dinner and go to a bar instead?" Anders asks.

"I'm in."

Anders often says the best thing about being an identical twin where one is gay and the other is straight is there's never any competition or rivalry. We make the best wingmen for each other because we have different targets.

That's his point of view. Mine? I see the guys Anders goes for and wonder what it would be like to be with a man just once.

I've had these thoughts since before Anders came out, but that rivalry Anders thinks isn't there? It's squashed beneath my straight façade.

It's not that I'm scared to come out or worried no one will support me. I have a gay brother, for crying out loud. This isn't "I can't accept myself." Statistically, I'm not alone. If someone's gay, they're gay. They like the same gender. End of story. The idea of someone liking more than one gender somehow gets twisted and confusing for people—like there always has to be one they like more, or they always end up picking a side. There's a difference between finding a person to spend the rest of your life with and choosing to be with a particular gender, but that's apparently too hard for some people to understand.

That's only one of the reasons I've kept quiet, though. Aside from the fact I've always been attracted to males and females, I've never felt the need to explore my bisexuality. I've definitely thought about it, and as time goes on, it's getting harder and harder to ignore, but until recently, I'd never contemplated going for it.

When you grow up as the exact replica of someone else, you do anything to stand apart from them. Anders understands this more than anyone.

In high school, I chose soccer so he tried out for basketball. I played guitar so he picked drama classes. I got tattoos, and he got piercings. He went into accounting, and I went into teaching. We've spent our whole lives trying to be different and find our own personalities, I see being with guys as *his* thing.

Maybe my reasons for staying closeted would be insignificant to most, but the way I see it, it's a balance issue.

Anders wasn't lying when he said I hadn't dated in a while. I've been with my share … and probably my brother's share as well. You know, for balance reasons. And while I like being with a woman—and enjoy it—the effort in maintaining a relationship is endless. I find it easy to meet women. Holding onto them, however … that's a whole other language—one I can't speak.

The appeal of a man is something I've never allowed myself to give into, and I sometimes wonder if that's what's holding me back with women. I won't be ready to settle down until I get it out of my system.

I want to know what it's like.

Especially when I see some guy grinding against my brother on the dance floor from my spot at the bar while I nurse a glass of scotch. I want to be the one—okay, no, I don't want to grind against the twink he's chosen for the night. When I imagine being with a guy, I think strong and built with hard muscles to run my tongue over …

Okay, that's enough imagining.

Anders never used to go for effeminate guys, but now they're his security blanket.

My eyes catch on a couple behind Anders and his … boy. Now, these guys are my type. Both have thick, muscular arms and chests that lead down to narrow hips. Long legs in tight jeans … my own pants get tighter as I watch the couple dance.

Two girls sidle up next to me, dragging my eyes from the dance floor. One has long brown hair, bright red lips, and wears a tight dress. The other is blonde and dressed in an ugly white blouse and pencil skirt as if she's come straight to the bar from the office. She's wearing minimal makeup but is kinda cute with her blonde curls falling around her face.

"Would you, maybe, wanna dance with us?" the brunette asks.

"Because you want to dance with a guy but don't want to be groped, and seeing as we're at a gay bar, you think I'm not into groping?"

They stare at me, mouths agape.

I lift my chin in the direction of the dance floor. "I'm here because my brother refuses to go to straight bars."

"That's a little unfair," the brunette says and pouts, stepping closer. "How do you pick up in a gay bar?"

I'm not here to pick up, but a distraction might be nice. I force a smile. "How about that dance?"

"You two go on ahead," the brunette says. "I just have to run to the bathroom. I'll be out there soon."

I turn to the blonde. "I guess it's just us."

She looks between her friend and me. "Y-you want to dance … with me?"

Her friend encourages us to go with a satisfied smirk, and I think I've just walked into a trap. Especially when the brunette heads for the bar, not the toilets.

I don't want to lead this woman on. She's cute and all, but I'm in a rut, and not the type that can be cured by fucking any woman that moves.

"I'm sorry about her," she yells over the music. "I just broke up with my boyfriend, and she convinced me to come out, but I said I didn't want to be set up. Hence the gay bar. Guess that backfired, huh?"

I lean in so she can hear me. "Your boyfriend's a dick."

She throws her head back and laughs.

"It's just a dance." I grab her hand and lead her to where my brother was before.

I can't see him anymore, and it wouldn't surprise me if he's snuck off for a quick BJ with that guy.

With my arms around this woman, I pull her close, but I don't grind against her. I'm not here for a hook-up. Especially a rebound situation. I honestly don't know if I can be bothered to make the effort.

Twenty seconds into our dance, Anders' friend bounces

up to us. He's a good six inches shorter than me and looks too young to be in a club.

"You're back." His boyish smile makes him look even younger.

And how drunk is he? My brother is wearing a blue shirt, and I'm wearing a black button-down.

Before I have the chance to tell him I'm not Anders, he's bumping the girl out of his way, standing on his tiptoes, and planting his mouth on mine. I try to step back, but his hands wrap around my waist and pull me against him.

His mouth is surprisingly soft for a guy, but the hint of stubble as it scrapes along my chin awakens something in me I didn't even know was there. I mean, I've suspected and fantasised about it, but now it's actually happening, there's no denying it.

When his tongue pushes past my lips, I freeze. I contemplate taking this and letting my tongue meet his. Yeah, he's not my type, and yeah, he thinks I'm Anders, but he is a guy, and it's just a kiss—

"What the fuck?" Anders' voice cuts through the loud space.

The guy steps back, his gaze flitting between me and my brother, and his hand flies to his mouth.

Anders squeezes my shoulder. "I'm sorry, bro."

"Isn't the first time someone's mistaken me for you," I say dryly and wipe my mouth.

"Twins?" the guy says, practically squealing.

"Don't get any ideas, Chris," Anders says. "He's straight. And we definitely aren't into twin fantasy shit."

Eww, hell no.

Chris pales. "I'm so sorry."

I shrug. "Don't sweat it."

"Thanks for being a good sport about this," Anders says. "Any other guy might've thrown a punch."

"You know that's not my style." I tell the kids who come through the doors of my dojo that the martial arts I teach is only to be used in defence. It would be hypocritical of me not to do the same.

"Okay, Chris, quick lesson for you," Anders says and points to his left eyebrow. "Pierced." He points to me. "Not pierced. Got it?"

Chris nods. "Got it."

Anders shoves him playfully. "Now, don't kiss my brother again, asshole." They disappear into the crowd of sweaty, half-naked guys, and I can never get over how different the start to Anders' flings are compared to a few weeks later when everything goes to shit.

He goes through the same motions, and it always ends the same. He goes from confident to unsure to panic attack mode, and he's as predictable as his breakups. I anticipate having to break up with Chris in a few weeks. Although, I don't know how that will work when Anders has given away our secret. Then again, Chris didn't exactly give us an option in this situation. I usually don't meet Anders' boyfriends until I'm breaking up with them. Anders stays at their place, and if he does ever have someone at our apartment, I'm exiled to my room and am referred to as the roommate.

The whole swapping places thing only works because his boyfriends don't know I exist. When Anders started getting me to do this for him a few years ago, he suggested I pierce my brow. That was going way past the line, and I told him to fuck off.

"Does that happen often?" the girl I'm with asks and steps closer. I should probably find out her name.

"First time I've been kissed by someone, but we get mistaken for each other all the time. Sometimes I think our parents can't even tell us apart. For all I know, I was born Anders and he's Law."

"Your name is Law?" she asks with a giggle.

"Lawson. Our parents wanted us to grow up to be lawyers or something. Anderson and Lawson sounds like a bloody law firm."

"They're cool names. My name is boring. It's Jodie."

"Thanks for the dance, Jodie, but I think I'm gonna head home. I've had a long day and an even longer night." And my shirt is still damp.

"No worries." Jodie takes off towards her friend, and I make a beeline to the exit.

It's a short walk home to our apartment, and I text Anders on the way, telling him I've gone home. He responds by calling me a pussy.

My brother, ladies and gentlemen.

Walking through the streets, I can't help thinking about my brief kiss with what's-his-face. It may've been short, but it's fuelled a fire. I want more. Not from him, but in general.

I can't ignore it anymore.

2
REED

This is the first and last time I let my neighbour set me up on a date. Deb is great. She let me use her Wi-Fi when I first moved into my apartment last week until I could set up my account. She knew I didn't know anyone in town and tried to set me up with her daughter. When I stammered, she said, "Oh, I'm guessing you were hoping I had a son instead." And that's how I ended up here, waiting at a restaurant for some guy who's not her son but her accountant. He's twenty minutes late.

I don't want to be here. I don't want to date again. Being dumped by your long-term boyfriend sucks. It's not great for my confidence or my ego to find out he was a lying asshole.

Welcome to Loserville. Population, me.

God, what if my blind date turned up, got one look at me, and then left? I stare down at my chinos, dress shirt, and sweater. Fuck, when did I start dressing like a teacher outside of the classroom too?

"Hi," a deep voice says beside me.

I'm met with brown eyes smiling down at me. "Anderson?" I ask.

From his closely trimmed beard to his wild, dark hair on top his head, he's about as close to the perfect male specimen as you could get. But by the look of his hoodie and jeans, I'm definitely overdressed.

The guy clears his throat and takes the seat opposite me. "I prefer Anders."

"I'm Reed."

"I know. My client said."

"I'm sorry about her. I'm new to Brisbane, and she kind of adopted me. Apparently that means she's comfortable enough to set me up with someone she doesn't know very well."

Anders smiles. "She did say 'You're gay, right? My new neighbour is gay. He's a teacher. You'd love him.'"

"Does she think you'd love me because I'm a teacher or because I'm also gay?"

"Who knows with straight people."

I laugh.

"Are you new to town or new to Queensland?" Anders asks. "Let me guess. Melbournite?"

Do I look like a pretentious hipster? "I grew up about two hours north of here. A small suburb on the Sunny Coast."

"Oh, so you're used to Queensland summers. They're hot as balls."

I snort. "And you're an accountant? No, offence, but you don't look like an accountant."

"You don't look like a teacher. A PE teacher, maybe."

What else does a guy do when he's not getting laid other

than work out? Maybe my breakup with Ben six months ago was for the better. With how Anders is eyeing me, I think it's definitely paid off.

"PE teachers are usually fat, so I take offence," I joke.

"I mean, you look fit." His eyes travel over my arms. "Muscly."

"You look *fit* yourself." It's been six long celibate months. I may not want a relationship, but I am a man.

"We ordering dinner?" he asks, his voice gruff.

"Sure. Or …"

"Or?"

"Or we could take it to go."

He swallows hard, and his Adam's apple bobs. "Or we could forget dinner completely."

"My place?"

Anders stands. "Lead the way."

We're out the door and on the street faster than physically possible. "It's two blocks in this direction," I say and tilt my head to the right.

We walk in hurried silence, the only sound being our feet on the pavement and the cars on the street. We make it a block before hesitance makes me wary. Now that we're doing this, he's gone quiet.

"You sure you want to do this?" I ask, because now I'm not so certain. He went from undressing me with his eyes to avoiding looking at me at all. "We don't have to—"

He spins on his heel and pushes me against the wall of the building, blanketing my body with his. Part of me wonders if I should be worried about the erratic move and how fast he's able to pin me down, but when I put my hands on his chest to push him away, he melts into my touch. He's an inch or two taller than me, so he stares down at me as he says, "I want to." The rawness of his voice makes any doubt disappear.

"Full disclosure? This is a hook-up. I can't offer any more than that." I decide to be straight up with him, because if he's not okay with this, I'd rather he bolted now.

"I'm good with hook-ups. I prefer them. I think my longest relationship was two months. Anders doesn't do forever."

"Does Anders often refer to himself in third person?" I ask.

"Sometimes. He can be a real douche."

"Good to know." I grip his shirt and pull him closer so our mouths are mere centimetres apart. I'll make him be the one to close the gap. I'm usually not into games or struggling for dominance—I like to give and take—but right now, I think he needs to be the one to take the lead. He was confident in agreeing to come home with me, but that fell away inch by inch with every step he took towards my apartment. It makes me wonder how many casual hook-ups he's had. If I had to guess, I'd say not many.

For a minute, I think he's going to resist, but then his mouth comes down on mine, strong and commanding.

His beard is softer against my mouth than I anticipated. He groans as he opens for me, and the sound goes straight to my cock. God, I need this. I didn't realise how much until right now. His tongue swirls with mine until I can't take it anymore.

"Apartment," I murmur.

"Uh-huh." He doesn't stop kissing me.

I pull him against me and rock my hips, pushing my

erection into him. "Apartment," I say again.

His mouth tears away from mine as he laces our fingers together. "Hurry."

Hand in hand, and in record time, we enter my building and climb the steps to the second floor.

I fumble with the keys as Anders kisses the back of my neck and his cock presses against my ass. When I manage to get the stupid door open, we stumble inside. He kicks the door shut with his foot as I spin and attack his mouth while walking backwards.

I grunt. This guy can kiss.

We bump into the kitchen island, so I wrap my arm around him and move us towards my bedroom, all the while our mouths not leaving one another.

His tongue is a mixture of domineering and exploring, while his lips and teeth are teasing. He goes from his tongue tangling with mine to his teeth grazing my lower lip.

My apartment is an open floor plan; the only thing separating my kitchen from my living room and bedroom is a mosaic glass feature wall.

We don't make it to my bedroom. I pull away from Anders and reach for the hem of my sweater to take it off. He watches intently as my hands move to the buttons of my shirt. "Shirt off," I order.

He pulls his hoodie and T-shirt off in one go. My eyes roam over his hard torso, his abs, and up to his shoulder where a black tribal tattoo covers his entire right pec and part of his arm.

"You really don't look like an accountant."

"I don't like stereotypes, so I make sure I don't act or

look like one." Reaching forward, he grabs my belt to bring me closer.

"Isn't having casual sex with someone you don't know a stereotype?"

Anders shrugs. "But it's the fun type."

"I love loopholes."

Our mouths find each other once more, and he backs me up to the glass partition, pushing me against it.

His hands undo my belt and pants, shoving them—along with my boxer briefs—down my thighs.

When his fingers wrap around my aching cock, I let out a shuddery breath.

"It's been so long for me, I'm going to blow in like a minute, but I promise I have at least another round, if not two, in me," I say.

His hand freezes on my cock for the briefest of moments as he eyes me. "How long has it been?"

"How long has it been for you?" I throw back.

"Answer at the same time? One, two … three."

We both say, "Six months" and then smile.

"We have all night," I say. "Let's just get this first one out of the way."

"How is a romantic guy like you still single?" His hand slowly picks up speed again, and I'm thankful his quip is rhetorical. Don't really want to open that can of worms mid-handjob.

His free hand undoes his jeans and drops them to the floor. No underwear helps.

"I love a man who can multitask." I throw my head back on the glass. Anders does this thing with his wrist on the upstroke, making my mind fuzzy and my balls heavy.

I want to cry when he takes his hand away, but then he raises it to my mouth. "Spit," he says.

Anders groans as I wet his hand then my own with saliva. He closes his eyes and shudders, his brow creasing in concentration.

His hand returns to my dick and I breathe deep through it, trying to hold onto any form of composure, but I'm literally about twenty seconds away from exploding all over the both of us.

Distraction. I need a distraction.

I wrap my fist around him and stroke. He leans into me, pinning me to the wall. The cold of the glass on my ass makes the heat between us burn hotter. He boxes me in, his left arm going above my head as his right keeps torturing me in the best way possible. His hips thrust forward, his dick fucking into my hand.

This isn't the distraction I was looking for. If anything, this is worse.

My head falls forward onto his tattooed shoulder, and I can't hold back from kissing the ink there.

He moans, deep and guttural, and his hips pick up their pace. "I'm going to …"

I nod against his shoulder. "Do it. It'll take me with you."

With a shudder and two more large thrusts, warmth fills my hand. He kisses a path from the bottom of my ear and down my neck while he continues to convulse.

"Fuck." I come harder than I have since I can't remember when, and I have to bite down on his shoulder to stop from yelling out.

I guess Anders likes it a bit rough, because when my

teeth sink into his skin, more spurts hit my hand.

We breathe heavy, not moving until we can compose ourselves.

"Shower?" I ask, but it comes out as a whisper.

"I don't know if my legs work."

I laugh. "They're holding you up pretty good."

"I think that's you."

In our haste, we only managed to get our pants to our ankles, so we step out of them, and I drag him towards my bathroom.

Anders stands awkwardly as I turn the faucet on and wait for the water to heat up. His body is insane. Long and muscular without being bulky. Tight abs, firm ass ... damn, I just hooked up with that.

Once we're under the spray, Anders furrows his brow as if deep in thought.

"What's up?" I ask.

"I need to tell you something."

"Not really what a guy likes to hear when he's washing your jizz off his stomach."

Anders laughs. "It's not bad. Okay, it's kinda bad. I ..." He turns his back to me and dips his head under the water. When he wipes his face, he continues to avoid eye contact as he says, "I ... I can't stay for round two. I need to go home."

"Oh, okay. Not to a wife or anything, right?"

His behaviour is sketchy, but he laughs it off. "No wife. Promise."

I was the one to say this would only be a hook-up, but I'd hoped for at least a few more hours with the guy.

Leaning forward, he lowers his head, and his mouth

claims mine in a soft, appreciative kiss—the complete opposite to ten minutes ago. "Thanks for the, uh …"

"Orgasm?"

He runs his hand over the back of his neck. "Uh, yeah."

I don't realise my hand has gone to his forearm to stop him from getting out of the shower until it's too late. "Look, I'm new here, I have only one friend—"

"My client?" he asks.

"Okay, so I have a whopping two friends here. Apart from a guy I went to high school with, I have no one. I know we said this would just be a hook-up, and I don't want more, but … could we, like, hang out or whatever?"

Anders runs his hand over his beard. "I don't know if that's a good idea, but the fact you were more confident asking me to fool around than you were at asking to hang out, I feel like I can't say no."

"That's how I get all my friends. I guilt them into it."

He smiles. "Okay, *friend*. I'll leave my number for you on your kitchen bench."

"I probably should've led with the friend thing and kept my pants on, but what can I say, you're hot. Hot guys don't make me think clearly."

"I'm hot, huh?"

"Extremely, but I think you already know that. I'll walk you out."

We towel off and dress quickly.

I don't bother putting on my shirt to walk him to the door, but Deb has impeccable timing. Or maybe she was out there all night, waiting to see how my date went. Considering Anders and I went straight to the sex part of the evening, she's probably been waiting for me to come home, not—"

"Anderson," she singsongs and then glances at me. Her eyes go from my bare chest then to his wet hair. She purses her lips. "You took your eyebrow piercing out."

Anders tenses. "Uh … I … umm …"

He has an eyebrow piercing? That's hot.

3
LAWSON

Where did this woman come from? The CIA? Or whatever Australia's equivalent of that is. This woman sees my brother once a year and she notices when he's not wearing jewellery?

"You have an eyebrow piercing?" Reed asks.

"I, uh, sometimes take it out for dates." I wince. I take it out for dates? What kind of lame-ass excuse is that? "Sorry, I need to get home."

I stumble down the hallway, but Reed shouts out, "You never left your number."

I know.

"Oh, I can give it to you," CIA woman says.

Shit.

I race back to them real fast. "That's my business number. Here, I'll give you my personal one." I hold out my hand.

Reed reaches into his pocket and produces his phone, and I feel physically ill typing my brother's name into it.

Idiot, idiot, idiot.

Hey, Law, can you go break off a date for me?

Sure. By break off, you mean jerk off, right?

I didn't plan this. Anders called me in the middle of a panic attack. Apparently, a client of his had set him up with a school teacher fresh out of uni, and Anders didn't expect him to be so … intimidating.

What kind of English lit teacher has a body like Reed? I told Anders he was stupid for accepting a blind date with his issues, but my brother likes to think with his dick. That is, until his head reminds him there are certain situations he can't handle.

Anders couldn't call or text to cancel because he didn't have Reed's number, and he physically couldn't bring himself to enter the restaurant, so I found myself running to him to break off the date. Anders was so shaken up, he couldn't even stay to watch. He filled me in about what happened and what I needed to know and then called a cab and left before I'd even entered the restaurant.

As soon as I saw Reed sitting there, I understood why Anders couldn't go through with it himself.

Reed isn't my brother's type. He would've been at one time, but that was years ago. Reed has muscles and that hard look about him. His square jaw is prominent and he has an adorable chin dimple. The most boyish thing about him is his golden hair and his ridiculous preppy boy clothes. The rest is all man.

If he let his facial hair grow, he'd look like the dude from *Sons of Anarchy* but in a sweater instead of leather.

The plan was to claim family emergency and walk away, and in all honesty, I should've checked on my brother.

Anders might've been hyperventilating into a paper bag for all I knew. But as soon as I sat down and Reed smiled at me? I was a goner.

I almost came clean in the shower—in the confessing sense, not the personal hygiene sense—but it was only a hook-up, and I figured I wasn't going to see the guy again.

Now he has my number, and Anders' client knows "he" hooked up with Reed.

Shit, shit, shit, shit, shit.

My freak out hasn't died down by the time I walk through the door, and Anders stares up at me from the couch. He pulls his wringing hands apart. It's a nervous habit he does that lets me know he's not handling shit well, so he always tries to hide it when I catch him doing it. "How did it go?" His voice cracks. "You were gone for ages."

"I ended up having dinner afterwards. He was actually a pretty decent guy." *Really decent. Looks hot naked, if you were wondering.*

God, what have I done?

Not that I regret a second of it. Does that make me a bad person? Isn't one of the commandments 'Thou shalt not lie about thy identity'? Wait, that might be in the gay rule book of things *to* do. Especially in a hook-up situation.

"I know you said you weren't going to do that for me anymore," Anders says quietly, "but—"

"It's okay," I say. "I understood why this time. Are you all right?"

Not that he'd tell me if he wasn't. Anders likes to pretend he has everything under control, and it's not until moments like tonight where he calls me completely breathless and in agony that I remember the demons from his past will never be gone. Especially when he refuses to go back to counselling for them.

"I'm good now. I curled into a ball and put on classic rock."

"KISS can cure anything."

Anders stands and approaches, giving me an awkward and rare brotherly hug. "I'm sorry, okay? I'm sorry for a lot of things, but I'm mainly sorry you have to keep bailing my ass out."

"I'm your brother. You know I'll do anything for you."

Anders grins.

"Oh, fuck. What did I just agree to do for you?"

"Come home with me this weekend to ask the 'rents for money to pay for therapy?"

I let out a relieved breath. I've been begging him for ages to go back. "I'm there. Although, it never ceases to amaze me that you're a broke accountant. You're a walking oxymoron."

"Hey, I'm great at budgeting."

"Just not great at sticking to it," I mumble. "I'd help you out myself but—"

"Pfft, you earn less than me. You should work at a gym as a personal trainer, or hell, buy your own gym. You'd earn more. Or, do what you originally set out to and become a real teacher. Private schools pay their teachers a shit load."

"I *am* a real teacher. Besides, I love my job."

"Do you, though? You're not doing it because you feel guilty about what happened—"

"I'm helping those kids. And you. That's all I need."

Most of the kids I work with are great, but it's the troubled teens I like working with most. When I get the chance to change someone's life, it fills me with a sense of accomplishment that no other job could. My dojo runs a program with the local schools, promoting anti-bullying, teaching self-defence, and giving these kids a much-needed boost in their confidence and self-esteem.

I may not have been able to help my brother, but I can prevent other kids like him from being a victim, and hopefully, stop other kids from being aggressors.

Anders stares at my head. "Why's your hair wet?"

Shit. "It, uh, rained on my way home."

He glances down at my dry clothes and then back up to my face.

"I'm going to go to bed," I say and practically bolt for my room. I pause in the doorway. "Anders?"

"Yeah?"

"When's the next time you see your client? The one who set you up tonight."

"Not until next year. We just finished her tax return. Why?"

Thank fuck. "Was wondering if I had to give you a play-by-play of tonight in case she asks."

"You let the guy down gently, didn't you?"

Making him come would be considered gently, right? "Of course. Uh … goodnight."

I make my way to the coffee machine faster than a sailor on a whorehouse. It's going to be a long day, and caffeine might not cut it.

Anders must think the same way because he sits at the kitchen table, staring at a prescription pill bottle.

"What are those?" I ask and silently will the coffee machine to warm up faster.

"Anti-anxiety pills I had left over from a while back. They're still in date."

"The ones that made you sick?"

Anders doesn't take his eyes off the bottle as he says, "They only made me sick because I was popping them like candy. I think one might help me fake it with the parentals —take the edge off."

Ah. The reason today is going to be long.

Elizabeth and Connor Steele are great parents. No one could ever dispute that. They are, however, melodramatic. To understate it. Especially Mum.

We both know what's going to happen when Anders asks for money. Dad will suggest a rehab facility for intensive treatment. Mum will suggest Anders move home. They'll both want to help in their own way, but Anders needs to do what he's comfortable with. Moving back to our hometown in northern New South Wales where everyone knows everyone's story, and where Mum can smother him twenty-four seven, won't do anything for his sanity. Alternatively, rehab is an intense quick fix that won't do any good for him in the long run.

Weekly therapy sessions work for Anders—when he goes —but it's something he's going to have to keep going to. Possibly forever. At one hundred fifty bucks a pop though, there's no way we can afford it.

"Maybe we shouldn't go," Anders says.

"They'll give you the money."

"That's not …" Anders grunts and runs a hand over his dark beard. "Do you know how shitty I feel about asking my mummy and daddy for a loan because my head is all messed up?"

Probably about the same amount of shittiness I feel about hooking up with my brother's date. The confession is on the tip of my tongue, but when Anders' hand shakes as he reaches for the bottle, I know now's not the time.

I pour both of us coffee and then slide into the seat opposite him. "What if you had cancer and needed money for meds or hospital visits or whatever?"

"But I don't have cancer."

"PTSD and anxiety are still medical issues that need treatment."

"I was doing better. I …" He sighs.

This is something he still doesn't understand—a lot of people don't. Conditions like his aren't curable, only manageable. And while he has been doing better, minus the fact he still can't deal with conflict, the truth is, I've seen the warning signs building for months. Each breakup is a little harder on him, and physical signs like the tremors and being withdrawn are getting worse. Add that to his panic attack over Reed …

"Just look at it this way. You've been out of therapy for, what, a year now? If you were a car, you'd go in for a service after a year, so pitch it to Mum and Dad that you need a check-up. And when your psychiatrist says you need to come back to regular sessions—which she will—tell our parents you're delving further into your issues because you're doing better. That'll get them off your back."

With another sigh but more resolve, Anders pops the cap on the bottle and swallows a pill dry.

"Bit early for it, isn't it?" Our drive will be almost two hours to Mum and Dad's place.

"We better get on the road, and God knows I need something to help me suffer your singing all the way there."

"Love you too, brother."

Anders stands. "Let's get this over with."

The anti-anxiety meds turn out to be a good thing for Anders because he sleeps most of the car ride there. It turns out to be bad for me, though, because it gives me alone time with my thoughts, and that's never a good thing. Especially when I can't get a certain blond teacher out of my head.

Maybe the mental image of him jerking me off should fill me with guilt, but all it does is make me wish I'd stayed for more. It's not like I can go back there. No matter how much his text this morning makes me want to. Wasn't anything major—just a simple *got plans this weekend?*

Yeah, I do. I'm going home with the guy you think you fooled around with but didn't.

And *that's* why I have to ignore him and move on.

I won't think of his hard chest, the rough stubble from his five o'clock shadow, or how I pinned him against the wall and fucked his hand. Nope. Not gonna think about that.

My dick has other ideas. I shift in the driver's seat to try to get comfortable, because driving with a hard-on is never fun.

Stop thinking about Reed.

Anders' snoring is a constant reminder he's beside me, so at least that helps deflate my cock.

As soon as I pull off the motorway for the Byron exit, Anders snorts so loud he wakes himself.

"Shit, we're here already?"

"Yup."

He throws his head back on his seat and shuts his eyes again, but I know he's not going back to sleep. He's trying to disappear.

I've been around Anders enough to know he doesn't need encouraging words right now. He needs tough love or silence, and seeing as today's going to be hard enough, I opt for silence.

Mum and Dad bought a house along the beachfront thirty years ago when property prices were insanely low. Now, the street where our childhood home sits is filled with beach mansions. They have high fences and no yards with private paths that lead to the beach.

Our house is still a shack, but it has the classic Byron hippie vibe. Our yard has surfboards lining the back fence instead of security cameras, and we have an actual lawn.

As soon as we pull into the driveway, Anders pulls out his eyebrow barbell.

"Really, man?" I ask. "We're still playing this game?"

He grins. "Wouldn't hurt to make them feel a little guilty about getting us mixed up before we ask them for money."

There's no fighting that logic.

When we climb out of the car, the scent of strawberries makes my mouth water. The fruit and veggie patch that lines our garden has fruit year-round thanks to the tropical climate. The smell reminds me of my childhood and running from the beach after a surf and scarfing down fresh fruit while Mum prepares dinner.

I breathe in deep and savour the salty air that's home. I've thought about moving back, but it's not a possibility. Not with Anders. Plus, I make more money in the city. More students to teach.

"My babies," Mum says from the front porch. She has love in her smile but worry in her eyes.

"We're twenty-eight," Anders grumbles.

It's not that we don't come home often—although we could probably step up the visits—but the fact she's a worrier. Her house may be on the hippie side, but she's far from the free-spirit persona this town was built on.

Mum hugs us both in a deathly grip.

When she pulls back, she cups my cheeks. "Anders, honey, I hope you got that rash cleared up. It's never good having a rash down there."

My eyes widen and then dart to Anders.

"Mum!" Anders snaps and turns to me. "She's lying."

She doesn't even try to cover her smugness. "Serves you right for trying to trick your mother, *Anderson*. Put your eyebrow ring back in. Your dad lost his glasses again, so he'll have no hope telling you apart."

"Oh, don't pull the mother knows everything card," Anders says. "You once dropped me at Law's soccer practice, thinking I was him."

"It's not my fault you both look alike."

Anders and I share a glance.

"Actually, Mum," I say, "I think the whole identical twin thing *is* your fault. I could give you a quick lesson in anatomy if you're still confused after all these years."

She waves me off. "Come out back. The barbecue's in full swing, and your father's burning the steaks."

Once Mum's walking away, Anders takes a deep breath.

I squeeze his shoulder. "We got this."

We don't even get lunch plated up before Dad says, "You need money."

"Can't we just come home because we miss you guys?" Anders asks.

Mum and Dad look at each other and then back at him. As if rehearsed, they both say, "No."

I try to hold in my laugh.

"Fine," Anders says. "Just, don't freak out, okay? I want to go back to therapy, and—"

"What happened?" our mother asks.

Yup, right on cue.

"Nothing happened," Anders says. "But it's been a while, and I've had a teeny, tiny, little bit of anxiety lately …"

Don't scoff. Do not rat your brother out. Rule number one as a twin—always have your brother's back, no matter what. Another rule: don't hook up with someone while pretending to be your brother.

Yeah, oops.

"I want to get on top of it before it becomes worse," Anders says.

Dad purses his lips. "You can take our emergency credit card." He puts up less of a fight than I expected, but Mum isn't so easy.

"Wouldn't it be best to move home and away from the toxicity of the city?"

Predictable as ever.

"I'm fine," Anders says. "I just need a few sessions to stay on top of things. And I'll pay you back."

"We know you will," Dad says. "And if you think this is what you need, then you know we'll help any way we can. Now eat up before your charcoal gets cold."

The overcooked meat is gamey and chewy.

"Is this cow?" Anders asks, staring at his steak.

"Roo," Mum says. "It's leaner and healthier."

"And grosser," Anders mumbles.

Never understood our nation's need to eat their own national emblem. Kangaroo meat tastes like ass.

"Law, are you seeing anyone?" Mum asks, and I almost choke on my food, but it's not because of how inedible it is.

The image of a certain blond flashes through my mind for about the tenth time today, but I ctrl, alt, delete that bitch.

Anders laughs. "He's more of a hermit than I am."

Mum's fork clatters to her plate. "Are … are you seeing someone?" she asks my brother.

Mum and Dad are unaware of Anders' manwhorish ways for good reason. They both stare at him with half-hopeful, half-concerned expressions. They want him to move on, but at the same time, they're terrified of him being hurt again.

Anders shrugs. "I've had a few dates. I'm trying to get back out there."

"Maybe that's why the anxiety's come back," Mum says quietly.

"It hasn't come back," I say. "It never left. It's not like he was cured and then caught it again. It'll always be there, and he'll always have triggers. Counselling helps keep it under control." I was going to bite my tongue, but this is why he asked me to come. I can run interference and stop Mum and Dad from ganging up on him.

Anders stares at me and gives a small nod in thanks.

"Have you thought about medication again?" Mum asks.

"I don't like how I feel on them. They make me numb to everything."

"Well, who are you dating? Is it serious? Maybe you're not ready." Our mum, the worrier.

"You want me to live as a monk forever?" Anders asks.

"Of course not," Mum says. "But maybe you should take things slow."

"It's been five years," Anders says.

Shit, has it really been that long?

Dad cuts in. "I think what your mother is trying to say is you don't have to push yourself if you're not ready."

Anders' hands wring together. "I *want* to be ready."

Mum and Dad might have their doubts, but the fact Anders is saying that out loud? It's a step I never thought I'd see him take. That has to be a good thing.

4
LAWSON

With mid-semester break over and everyone back at school, the dojo is quiet during the day. I have early morning classes before school, and then I do my daily workout and plan lessons. Come three p.m., I have back-to-back classes until six.

It's long hours, but I get to do something I love every day and get paid for it. I'm not rolling in money, but it pays my bills. Of course, if my brother ever decides to move out, I'm screwed and would need a new roommate, but I don't see Anders being on his own any time soon.

My first class of the afternoon is a program I run with the local schools. Each day, a different school brings the kids from their LGBTQ union in for self-defence classes that the schools pay for, so the kids get free lessons.

I wish we lived in a world where this wasn't an issue—ideally *no one* should have to learn to protect themselves—but I'm an advocate of doing whatever it takes to make sure none of these kids becomes a victim. Until we can fix the world, people have to protect themselves, and I hope they never have to use what I teach them.

I run a little late on my workout, so when it's time for today's school to arrive, I'm sweaty and still putting away equipment and setting up the mats for class.

The door to the shopfront opens with a jingle, and the sound of teens echoes through the space as if they're all yelling into a loudspeaker. How are kids so loud? I get they're excited and they're kids, but I mean, physically, how are they so loud?

One good thing about teaching Japanese martial arts—a mixture of judo, karate, and aikido—I get to tell the kids the dojo is a quiet space. It works about half the time.

I'm almost finished setting up when someone steps through the small opening separating me from the reception area by only a bamboo curtain.

"Anders?"

I bolt upright and freeze at the sight of Reed standing in my doorway. How did he find me? Wait ... he called me Anders, and he looks as surprised as I do.

"Mr. Garvey?" One of the kids enters the room behind Reed, wearing his gi. "Hi, Law." Davis bows with a palm to fist out in front of him. I'm supposed to bow back, but I'm stuck blinking at Reed.

"Law?" Reed asks.

"I'm Lawson Steele." I clear my throat. "Anders is my brother."

"Holy shi—vers."

"Mr. Garvey almost said shit!" Davis runs out to the other students like it's the biggest news of the year.

"Reed Garvey. I, uh—"

I take his outstretched hand and shake it. The hand that —nope, don't go there. "You went out with Anders?"

Reed lets out a relieved breath. "Thank God. I thought I might've been dangerously close to outing him to his twin brother."

I laugh, but it's forced. "Anders has been out since high school. You're safe."

"I, uh, had a date with Anders last week."

"Let me guess, you haven't heard from him since."

Reed laughs. "You would be correct."

We stare each other down to the point of awkwardness, and survival mode kicks in. All I'm picturing right now is last weekend, pushing this guy against the wall in his apartment, and having the most explosive sexual encounter of my life. And it was only a fucking handjob. What would happen if …

Nope. Seriously, don't go there.

Knowing I'm about to have a room full of teenagers, I quickly think of something to deflate the tightness in my pants and the memories of that night. The last thing I want to do is have a hard-on while working with kids.

Can anyone say prison time?

And it's not like my gi hides anything.

Even though I'm not aware of it, I manage to get out a normal sentence. "What happened to that Jenkins lady from Carindale High?" Give me a fucking medal, please.

"I think Carindale was excited to have a gay teacher to take over the LGBTQ union when I got the job," Reed says. "And then as soon as I found out about this program, there was no holding me back. I wish I had something like this in high school."

"That's why I established it," I say.

Reed cocks his head.

"For Anders." *And me, but no one knows about that.*

"Right. Of course."

"I better …" I nod in the direction of reception where the kids are getting louder by the second. "You're welcome to stay and watch. Or go to the coffee shop up the road. That's what Mrs. Jenkins did."

"I'll stay. I mean, I'd like to watch, if that's okay. I want these guys to know I'm not here because I have to be—that I want to be here and if they need help or advice or whatever …"

"You could even join in if you really want." I grin.

"The kids will love that."

I don't say aloud that I wouldn't mind it either.

Reed takes up a spot in the back, but the kids won't have that. Especially after I point out their new teacher is joining in.

After Reed takes his place next to me as my "assistant" and sends me a glare, I wink at him and start with stretches and light warm-ups. Then we move on to the routine katas I teach each week.

Reed's eyes stay on me the whole class, and I can tell it's not just in an observatory way. Pretty sure he doesn't give a shit if he's getting the movements correct. Maybe I'm reading into it, because it was me the other night who Reed had his mouth all over, not my brother like he thinks. Maybe he *knows* it was me. I shake that thought free. There's no possible way he could know.

The two messages Reed's sent me since then have gone

unanswered, even though I've desperately wanted to see him again. My right hand is no replacement for Reed's.

It might've been the fact it'd been six months since I'd had sex with anyone, or maybe it's because it was my first time with a guy, but I swear I've never come so hard in my life.

I want a repeat but have refrained for two reasons. He thinks I'm Anders, and he's after friendship, not a fuck buddy situation, and that's all I could offer right now. Even though I've always known I'm attracted to males as well as females, I don't know if I could see myself with a guy long-term. Maybe it's my Anders hang-up about us needing to be different to one another, or maybe I have the old-school mentality that life equals marriage, babies, and a family, because that's the thing you do. If someone were to ask me why that's the thing to do though, I don't think I'd be able to find an answer. To populate the earth? Think we have enough people doing that already, and it's not always for the good of humanity.

My issue is, if I don't even know what I want in a partner, I'm certainly not going to go around announcing to my entire family I like dick, only to end up with women for the rest of my life. It's easier to keep my preferences quiet until I can work out exactly what they are on my own.

But a hand—pun totally intended—from Reed would be okay with me. If he was into it. Which he won't be if he finds out Anders isn't me. No, that I'm not Anders. Fuck, I'm even confusing myself.

After I take the kids through the routine, I get them to pair off and spar, while I stand at the front of the class and watch their technique and make sure they're not goofing off or actually hitting each other.

"You're a great teacher," Reed says beside me as he watches too.

"Thanks," I murmur.

"No, seriously. They listen to you. They respect you."

"Probably because they see me as one of them. I have the maturity of a fifteen-year-old."

"I think it has more to do with the fact you look badass and have a black belt," Reed says.

I look badass? Awesome. "Might also be that I'm teaching them something they can use in the future. They see value in it."

He mock gasps. "Are you saying the English I teach these kids is not usable?"

"Have you seen how these lot communicate with each other? With the OMGs and the WTFs. What happened to good old-fashioned *what the fuck*?"

Reed glances at our class who keep continuing what they're doing and ignore me. "Okay, seriously, how did you not get a reaction to that?"

I lean in. "I'm magic."

Davis snorts in the front row, and when I cock my brow at him, the smile drops from his face.

"See. Magic."

"I don't know whether to be in awe of you or hate you right now."

"You'll get the hang of it. You're new to it, right?"

"God, is it that obvious?"

Fuck. I'm not supposed to know anything about this guy. "No, you look young, is all."

"I can't be any younger than you."

"Did Anders tell you we were twenty-three?" What am I saying? I know I didn't tell him that.

"Does he lie about his age often?"

"Always."

"He never said how old, actually."

"Twenty-eight. He's ten minutes older."

Reed's eyebrows shoot up in surprise. "I never would've guessed you guys were nearly thirty."

I scowl. "Hey, cut it with that thirty shit."

"Sorry," Reed says and tries not to smile. He fails.

"Is this your first teaching job?"

"I've been subbing the last six months since graduating, but a spot opened up with Carindale, so I moved from the Sunny Coast, and here I am."

"So, you're twenty-three?"

"Twenty-four. I did the four-year English degree and then the extra year to get my teaching qualifications."

Davis starts to get sloppy in his attacks, and his partner —a quiet girl whose name I can never remember—is hitting harder to retaliate, and if he doesn't cut it out soon, he's going to cop a knife-strike to his face.

"Davis," I snap. "Watch your form."

The wiseass salutes me.

I lean in and whisper to Reed. "I know we're not supposed to have favourites, but if I was allowed …" I tip my head in Davis's direction.

"I haven't had a class with him yet," he whispers back, "but I was warned he was disruptive and acts out a lot."

"That's why I like the kid. Reminds me of me." If I didn't know for a fact I wasn't Davis's dad—having been thirteen when he was born—I'd have to wonder. I swear the kid is me when I was his age. Even down to his dark hair, brown eyes, and lanky form he hasn't quite grown into yet.

I have to wonder if it's karma sending a student to me who's a bigger smartass than I am.

Before I'm ready, I have to pull myself away and finish the class the way I always do—by getting the kids to attack me as if I were a real attacker.

"Who haven't I picked on for a while?" As I ask this, the shy girl turns to avoid eye contact. Her little mouth moves frantically as if chanting, *not me, not me, not me*, and that's when I remember her name. "Chantel. You're up."

She shuffles her way into the middle of the room where they've all made a circle.

"Okay, I'm going to get you into a choke hold, and I want you to get out of it," I say.

"I'll never be able to do that."

"Yes, you will. You just need practice. I'm going to keep doing it until you get me on the ground. I don't care if it takes all night, I cancel the rest of my classes, and all these guys go starving because they don't make it home to dinner on time."

Sometimes the kids need a little push. It can backfire, but Chantel is the type of girl who wants to stay out of the spotlight. By keeping her peers happy, she'll be left alone.

I know Reed watches me the whole time without having to look at him.

It takes Chantel four tries, but then she nails the move, and I go down with a loud "Oomph."

The rest of the small class of ten cheer for her while I catch my breath. When I stand, I hold out my hand for a high five, and she slaps it with the most enthusiasm I think is possible for an introvert.

"Next week, I expect you to get it first try."

That makes her smile fall.

"You just proved you can do it, kid." I hunch over, still trying to get air back in my lungs. She winded me when I hit the mats, but I don't care about being hurt.

I pick on two more kids before the class finishes, and when it's over, Reed turns to me as the kids file out the door.

"What time do you finish up here?" he asks.

"Six."

"Would you … I mean, I assume you're straight so this isn't me hitting on you, but would you want to go to dinner or for a beer afterwards? The only person I've met since moving here is Anders. And, well, I may've fucked that up, because he's ignoring me."

The under-five's class starts pouring in, and Elise, a little girl with blonde pigtails, runs up and punches me in the leg. Reed tries to hide a laugh. For a four-year-old, she packs a hit, and I have to grit my teeth to stop from swearing.

"Elise, honey, no," her mother says and gives me that flirtatious smile she does every week. I'm not stupid enough to hit on the single mothers who pay me to teach their kids karate, so I give her a non-flirtatious wave back.

I'm too distracted and don't have time to go over why it's a horrible idea or come up with an excuse not to go out with Reed after work. "I could do dinner," I say.

"Meet you back here at six?"

I nod.

What the fuck am I doing?

5

REED

Sitting across from a guy who I've hooked up with when I haven't actually hooked up with him is the weirdest thing ever. The noise of the pub is drowned out around us as we wait for our food and I study Law.

He eyes me warily. "Why are you looking at me like that?"

"Sorry. The resemblance is uncanny."

He goes to open his mouth, but I cut him off.

"I'm not a dumbass. I know how the whole identical twin thing works. But there's usually some differences, even if they're subtle."

"Anders has his eyebrow pierced if that helps. That's usually how we're told apart."

"He wasn't wearing it when I went out with him."

Law flattens his lips into a thin line. "I'm going to be honest with you, and you shouldn't take offence to this, but … you're not his usual type."

"Maybe that's why he's ignoring my texts."

"Don't take it personally."

"I'm not. We had fun. Wouldn't mind a repeat, but I'm not going to chase a guy who's not interested. I'm not that pathetic." I sip my beer. "Just thought I should clarify that seeing as I kinda ambushed you into having dinner with me. I might've scared your brother off with that too—doing the whole grade school *will you be my friend* shtick. I've never been smooth."

"You don't have a lot of friends?"

"Not here. I come from up north, and a buddy of mine from high school moved down here for uni and never came back, but he's the only person I know, and I haven't managed to catch up with him yet."

"I'll only be your friend if you ask me on a piece of paper with boxes saying yes or no."

I laugh. "Wow, you really are old. Don't you know it doesn't count unless it's Facebook official?"

"Ah. The Facebook."

I like how easy it is to laugh with Law—I haven't had that with someone in a really long time—but I still can't help thinking about his brother. "Can I ask one thing about the twin thing? I promise I'll drop it after that."

"Shoot."

"Why the beard? I mean, do you two try to look exactly the same on purpose?"

Law's hand rakes over his facial hair, along his jaw, and down to his chin. Even his mannerisms are like Anders'. "Honestly? One hundred percent truth here? I hate the beard."

I smile.

"But I can't bring myself to get rid of it, and neither can Anders. It's a long story."

"I teach English for a living. I like stories."

"You a writer?" Law asks.

"Tried to be. I started a lot of stories but never finished any. I have a lot of unwritten things up here." I point to my head. "You know what they say, those who can't do, teach."

"Not true in my case. I've won a ton of martial arts trophies. Was even in contention to represent Australia at the Olympics in judo at one point." A cocky grin takes over his face, and for a split second I see that same grin as it looked down on me last weekend. Right before he kissed me … err, Anders kissed me.

Okay, this might be too weird for me, but what other choice do I have in the friend department? All the other teachers at Carindale High are ancient.

"What made you want to teach kids?" I ask.

Law shifts in his seat and avoids eye contact. "The plan was to become a high school teacher like you. Got my BA, and then … you know how there's one event in everyone's life that they measure everything against? Like, a parent dying or maybe in your case coming out; nine-eleven for most Americans. Lives are split down the middle and referred to as before the incident and after it."

I nod. "My parents died when I was seventeen. Car crash. I didn't get the chance to come out to them, but I think they would've been cool with it. They were always the type of parents who told my sister and me to be whatever and whoever we wanted."

"Shit. Sorry. Didn't mean to put that on you just now." Law seems flustered and uncomfortable.

"It's okay. It was a long time ago, and I've dealt with it."

"Umm, well my thing made me want to do something positive and make a difference, and the only way I know how to do it is by giving kids the opportunity Anders never had. I might not be changing the world, but I'm helping kids protect themselves from it."

"It must've been traumatic—what happened to Anders." My mind jumps to the worst possible conclusions, and the fact Law isn't elaborating, I know I shouldn't push for more.

"There's a lot of words to describe it. Traumatic would be one of them. It makes me protective of my brother."

I try to smile. "Oh, so that's what this is? You agreed to come to dinner to make sure my intentions are honourable."

"No. Just letting you know I'd do anything for Anders."

"It must be nice to be close to your family. When Mum and Dad died, my sister took her inheritance to travel the world. A few months turned into a year, and then a year turned into moving to Europe permanently. We've become the type of family where we message on birthdays and promise to make the trip to see each other at Christmas, but something always stops us. She's always broke, and while I'm smart enough to have saved most of my inheritance, trips to Europe are expensive." I've paid for that trip three times—twice for me and once so dipshit fuckface could come with me to meet my sister. You know, back when it was me and him forever and all that other bullshit he said. I swallow hard and push Ben from my mind—he doesn't belong there anymore.

"I live with Anders. There's no escaping him," Law says.

"From the short amount of time I spent with Anders, that doesn't seem like it'd be a hardship."

Law smiles but it falls just as fast. He opens his mouth to say something but stops himself. With a sip of beer for courage, he goes to try again but is interrupted by our dinner being served.

"Is there something you're not telling me?" I ask and shove a fry in my mouth. "Did Anders say something about—"

"Nothing like that. Don't mind me."

"Oh. O-okay …"

"Fuck," Law hisses. "I'm debating whether to tell you to stay away from Anders or not. He did talk about you. He had fun. But … the situation is—"

"You don't have to say anymore. If you want me to stay away from Anders, I will."

"I … no, don't do that. Ignore me. Anders is a big boy and can make his own decisions. I think."

I can't stop the laugh that flies out of me. "How about this? We don't talk about your brother at all. I doubt he's going to return my texts anyway."

"It won't be weird for you, being friends with me after …?"

I shrug. "I was okay with being friends with Anders after we hooked up, so being friends with someone who looks exactly like him isn't going to bother me."

"Okay, I know why my brother doesn't do long-term relationships. Why don't you?"

"Not against them. Had one all through uni. Now I'm free of it, I don't want to be tied down." Wow, way to understate getting my heart ripped out, but Law doesn't need to know the details.

"Bad breakup?"

Well, fuck. "Eh. I'd rather talk about how in the world you get those kids to do everything you say. Granted, today was my first day, and I've come in halfway through the school year so there's going to be hazing, but do they have to be so blunt?"

Law winces. "First impressions, man. You're fucked."

"Thanks."

"I think the biggest mistakes new teachers make is they want the kids to respect them, so they try to be tough. You know, do the whole 'You have to earn it' thing. I think if you give them respect from the beginning—tell them your opinion of each and every one of them right now is the highest it'll ever be—they'll do anything to stay up there. It's easier to hold onto something than build it from the ground up. Treat them like adults because all these teens want to do is be an adult. Why, I have no idea, but that's on them. They'll learn soon enough adulthood isn't all fun and games. When you're an adult, you don't have someone telling you to put on pants every day. You have to remember that shit on your own."

"That's the hardest part of adulting for you? Remembering pants?"

"The struggle is real."

"Okay, so you think being strong with the kids is the wrong approach? Everything we're taught in uni—"

Law scoffs. "Yeah, because learning how to teach kids in a room full of adults is the way to go. Most of my lecturers never saw the inside of an actual classroom other than the lecture halls at uni. They went from studying to professing … professoring? You're an English teacher, help me out here."

"Professoring is not a word, but I'm going to make it one."

"The professors themselves never taught a group of school-aged kids. They know shit all."

"So, I should just forget my four years of training and my degree?"

"Yup."

"Are you always this sunny and positive?"

"*Always*. I'm fucking delightful—a ray of sunshine and all that."

"What would you have taught if you didn't go into martial arts?" I ask.

"Sciences. Math, maybe. No English department would hire me. I can't tell my contractions from my adjectives. Verbs I'm good with because they're doing words. Which means they're fucking words, and that's how I remember them."

"I'll remember to teach the fifteen-year-olds that one."

"That'll be a way to get them on your side. Making a fool out of yourself this afternoon in class would've helped too."

"Please, Obi Wan, teach me everything you know." I'm ashamed to admit that the glimmer in his eye has my cock wanting to salute him.

Nope. Wrong brother.

Maybe being friends with Law will be hard after all, but after the brutal day I had today, I need all the teaching tips I can get.

I don't want to admit aloud that the kids in my classes today owned me. I'm a new teacher, taking over from someone who took a leave of absence because of bad health and was forced to retire early. I'm young, and the monsters saw an easy target and went for it.

They didn't listen, no one contributed to the discussions I tried to start, and one class even decided to publicly dissect my sexuality when one of the girls asked if I had a girlfriend and a boy muttered, "If she had a dick, maybe."

Of course, when I asked him what he said, he claimed he didn't say anything, but it was all out there now. It doesn't matter if the kids know I'm gay. I'm not hiding it, and the school board and everyone who needs to know is well aware of it. But it's the disrespect, and now that kid knows he can get away with it.

I've been subbing for the last six months, so I've had my fair share of dealing with rowdy kids taking advantage of me, but this is my first permanent position, and I think it's safe to say, after today, I'm fucking fucked.

"No offence, but you look like you're going to puke," Law says.

"Yeah, I'm just thinking about how they're going to eat me alive tomorrow."

"Lead with the verb joke."

"Sure, because joking about sex won't get me fired or anything."

Reed: *I WANT TO KISS YOUR BROTHER. I GUESS IF YOU AND I HAD SPOKEN INSTEAD OF HOOKED UP, I WOULD'VE FOUND OUT YOU HAVE A TWIN BROTHER WHO'S A TEACHER. SMALL WORLD, RIGHT? ANYWAY, HE GAVE ME SOME POINTERS AND I HAD A MUCH BETTER SECOND DAY AT WORK.*

Wanted to tell him thanks, when I realised I don't have his number. Hope this is okay, because I know he lives with you. I'm not a crazy stalker, I swear.

I'm not a crazy stalker? Who says things like that? Right—crazy stalkerish people.

Anders: *I dunno. Only crazy people think my brother is wisdomous and shit.*

Reed: *He speaks! Err ... texts.*

Anders: *Uh, yeah. Sorry for ghosting on you. I know you're new in town, but now you have Law, right?*

Reed: *I think I need aloe for that burn.*

Anders: *I mean because you guys have more in common.*

Reed: *Shame he's the straight brother.*

Anders: *Sorry.*

Reed: *Don't be sorry. It's cool. I'm not your type, and you don't want a repeat. Even if it's no strings ...*

Anders: *Tempting, but it's not a good idea.*

Reed: *Fair enough. Worth a try. Pass my thanks on to Law for me.*

Anders: *Will do.*

Maybe I should try Grindr or one of those dating apps to meet possible hook-ups. I don't want to date, but ever since Anders, I've never been hornier in my life. Turns out, he was the cure for my post-breakup lack of libido. Don't know if I'm quite that desperate for a hook-up app, though.

Not yet.

6

LAWSON

I'm going to come clean. That's the plan as I enter Reed's building and head up to the second floor. I'll lay it all out there and tell him everything:

I was the one he hooked up with.

It's me he's been texting.

I'm not straight. I'm bi.

I want no strings attached sex with him while I figure this whole thing out.

I am not my brother and never have been …

But then he's going to ask why, and the only response I'll have is because of reasons I can't say. Fuck. This isn't going to work. He'll want to know why I was the one who turned up for their date and not Anders. I won't betray my brother like that.

Oh, so pretending to be him is okay, but telling someone Anders was almost killed is crossing a line?

"Shit," I hiss under my breath and lean against Reed's doorjamb.

Damn, hardwood floors and long corridors make noise travel. Before I know it, and before I have time to retreat, Reed's door flies open.

There he stands, wearing a lime-green polo shirt and jeans, looking hot enough to fuck, and my mouth decides it's not time to cooperate.

Tell him.

Reed steps forward and yanks me into his apartment, closing the door with a slam. Fisting my shirt, he pulls me against him. For a small window, I think he knows it's me and not Anders. It's as if all the things I need to say are understood without me having to open my mouth. Wishful thinking, obviously, because when he closes his mouth over mine, I'm no longer able to tell him anything. And when he murmurs, "Thank fuck, you changed your mind," I know my delusion isn't real. He still thinks I'm Anders, and I'm going to let him continue to think it.

I've never understood people who cheat on a partner until now. While this isn't cheating, it is wrong, and I thought my conscience would be yelling at me to stop. Never have I been able to turn off that side of my brain, but as Reed's tongue pushes into my mouth, there's nothing but him and me and the promise of everything I've wanted for as long as I can remember.

With women, I've always been the dominant one—the one in control—but right now, I'm ready to throw every ounce of restraint out the window. Reed can take it all.

"I want you to fuck me," he says against my lips.

The command has my balls tightening. "O-okay." I sound unsure—too unsure.

Reed pulls back. "You down for that? I mean, I could go

either way if you prefer ... I'm an equal opportunist." He winks.

I grab his hips and bring him against me, determined not to let this opportunity pass me by because of nerves. "I want to fuck you, but you have to do something for me."

"What's that?" Reed smirks.

"I need you to tell me exactly what you like."

He leans in, his smile never wavering, and whispers, "Everything."

"Get specific. Tell me what you want me to do. And use your teacher voice."

"You have a teacher fantasy?" Reed's eyes glimmer.

"If I do?" I don't really, but this could be a fun way to learn a few tricks. And if Reed finds it weird that Anders has a teacher fetish when his twin brother is one, he doesn't say anything. Thankfully.

"You better get to work by undressing me." Reed's voice is exactly what I want. Rough, confident, and so damn hot.

I reach for the hem of his shirt, but before I can lift it off him, he stops me.

"Slowly."

I grin. I could so get into this game.

Leaning forward, I kiss him as my hands trail up his sides and my fingers run over his stomach. When I reach higher, he lifts his arms and we're forced to pull apart, but as soon as his shirt hits the floor, our mouths come back to one another—exploring, devouring.

Reed's arms wrap around my back as I reach for his belt and slowly loosen it. I hook my fingers into the waistband of his jeans and underwear.

"Nuh-uh," he says. "Jeans only." Once they hit the floor,

Reed's hand pushes down on my shoulder. "Take the rest off with your teeth."

"You're really getting into this bossy thing, aren't you?" I drop to my knees.

He groans as I tongue the hard planes of his abs, and his hand fists in my hair. His cock tries to push its way out of his tight boxer briefs, and even though the nerves have only intensified, adrenaline is now outweighing the insecurities over never having done this with a guy before. All I want to do is rip the rest of his clothes off and bury myself in him. My hands skim up his powerful thighs, but Reed grabs my wrists and holds them to his chest.

"No hands," he orders.

I moan, because I want him naked as soon as possible, and only using my mouth is hard. I kiss my way down his left side and grip his briefs between my teeth. When I only manage to get them halfway down his ass, he huffs.

"Screw this. I'm too impatient." He releases my hands and yanks off his underwear.

I have to laugh because it hadn't even been ten seconds of trying.

When his hand goes into my hair, he grips it close to the root so he has full control. "Suck me into your mouth."

Yes. This is what I want—what I've wanted for so damn long. My mouth wraps around his tight, salty skin.

"Just the tip," he says.

My tongue runs over his slit and precum fills my mouth. At the taste, my own cock leaks and begs for action.

Reed guides himself into my mouth in short and slow movements, allowing me to get used to him. "Fuck, cup my balls."

I do as he says and almost come when he thrusts harder into my mouth. He restrains himself so he's not forcing deep throat action on me, but his hips pick up speed as he moves in and out.

"Suck harder," he says, but as soon as I do, he swears under his breath and pulls out. "Wait, bad idea. I want you in my ass when I come."

I groan. "Bloody hell. At this rate, I'm going to come in my pants and we won't have that opportunity."

Reed smiles and widens his stance. Gripping my hand, he brings it to my mouth. "Suck."

I coat my fingers in as much salvia as I can manage, and when I glance up, Reed gives me the nod. He guides my mouth back to his cock as my fingers find his crease and press against his hole. I work my middle finger down to the knuckle and watch Reed for a reaction.

He throws his head back, and his ass clenches around my finger. There's no way I'm going to last more than thirty seconds inside him. He's hot and tight, so much so I'm surprised when he says, "More."

I've thought about bottoming before. I've always been curious, but adding a second finger inside Reed, I can't help wondering how it doesn't hurt.

Everything changes when my fingers hit that spongey spot inside him. I've tried to find my own prostate, but it's hard to get my finger high enough. No way am I risking buying a toy and having Anders find it in our apartment, and I haven't been comfortable enough with any of the women I've been with to ask them to experiment.

"Fuck," Reed hisses. "Scissor your fingers. Stretch me."

His hips piston, and his cock goes to the back of my

throat. I almost choke and gag but remind myself to breathe through my nose. My fingers work him over, massaging his prostate until he's grunting and fucking my face at a tempo I'm barely able to keep up with.

"Wait, wait, wait," Reed says. "I'm too close."

Part of me wants to say fuck it and let him come in my mouth, but the bigger part knows this can't happen again, and I only have this chance to get everything I can from Reed. I'll allow myself to have this night, and then when it's done, Anders will disappear from Reed's life and I'll be his colleague and nothing more.

Reed pulls out and puts distance between us by lying back on his bed. He takes his cock in his hand and strokes slowly. If someone had told me a month ago I'd be hooking up with a hot blond and watching as they touched themselves, Reed is the furthest thing I would have imagined. "Strip," he orders.

My shirt comes off without any finesse and then my jeans. Reed doesn't take his eyes off me as he reaches over to his bedside table and pulls out lube and a condom. He scoots to the end of the bed and pulls down my briefs.

Staring up at me with a devilish smirk, he says, "Don't come," and then engulfs my cock to the base in his wet, eager mouth.

Fuck, he wants me not to come? Not going to happen if he keeps that up.

My balls ache for release while my cock has found its nirvana. Reed moans, and the vibration does absolutely nothing to pull me back from the edge. I'm going to blow.

"You're evil," I pant and force myself to step away.

His smile is knowing; he's loving that I'm on my last

thread of control. "It's payback for almost making me come down your throat."

At least I can't say I suck at blowjobs … Actually, I do suck, if I want to get technical.

"You're supposed to be the one in charge here, so that's on you," I say.

Reed pulls me down on top of him and fuses his mouth to mine. His hands fumble between us, struggling to get the condom on me.

I don't want to stop kissing him, but he practically pushes me off him.

"Someone's impatient," I say as I rise to my knees.

"I need you in me." He rolls down the condom and passes over the lube, and I slather it generously.

"Are you ready for me?"

His eyes rake downwards and then back up to my face. "It's been a while, and you're not exactly small … It's one thing to feel full, but it's another ballgame being split in two."

Grinning, I add lube to my fingers as he spreads his legs and lifts his knees. I stroke his cock with my free hand when I go back to stretching him, but he's still insanely tight around my fingers. I'm mesmerised, watching my hand do to him what I've only ever done to myself.

Reed writhes beneath me, his eyes closed, his chest rising and falling in shallow pants, and I can't help wondering what it would feel like to be him right now. His lips part, and the look on his face expresses nothing less than heat and desire in a state of want. With a nod, he breathes, "I'm ready. Fuck, I'm so ready."

I don't think he is … I mean, if he is, this is all going to be over as soon as I'm inside him. Forcing myself to go slow so I don't blow my load early and to make sure he truly is ready, I line my cock up with his ass and ease my way in.

His hips buck, pulling me in farther, and I have to mentally run through a routine kata in my head to distract me from the zing shooting down my spine. When I'm fully seated, I have to pause.

"Move," Reed grunts.

"Can't."

Reed laughs and cups my cheek, bringing my face down close to his. "Breathe. And then fuck me."

My lips twitch. "Yes, sir."

He screws up his nose. "That's taking the fantasy a little too far. The kids at school sometimes call me that, so that's where I draw the line."

I laugh, and the small movement sends ripples down to my toes. "Sorry, teach."

"That's not any better," he says. "You good to go now?"

When I give a small nod, he pulls my face down and kisses me hard as I thrust in and out of him.

My muscles ache, and a light sheen of sweat drips down my body. Every time my hips connect with Reed's ass, the closer I get to losing any control I'm pretending to maintain.

If I thought Reed's mouth was heaven, it's nothing compared to his tight ass.

"I need …" he pants, "I need you to …"

He's unable to get the sentence out, and I realise he needs more from me. I straighten up, and my hand goes to his cock, stroking in time with my hips.

"Come with me," he says. "I'm really fucking close."

"Tell me when," I grunt, but he doesn't get the chance

to before his ass clamps down on my dick and I'm shouting out as I come. "Fuck!" I keep going, pushing my body past its limits, and when warmth fills my hand, I swear I come some more.

He convulses beneath me, writhing and cursing. I know he's going to say my name—it's on the tip of his tongue—but when he does, reality slams into me harder than my orgasm, and his raspy voice almost kills me.

"*Anders.*"

7
REED

I've barely recovered when Anders climbs out of bed. He's wobbly on his feet and catches himself by gripping the comforter.

"I'm not that much of an asshole," I say. "You don't have to run off right away."

"Thanks, but yeah, I kinda do." He scrambles for his clothes. "I shouldn't have come here."

Ouch. It's not like I want to marry the guy, but really? Can't even hang out for five minutes after getting off? If I didn't know any better, I'd worry Anders was some closet case, but that can't be right when Law knows all about it.

"Am I allowed to ask why?" I ask.

"You're friends with my brother." He doesn't look at me as he dumps the condom in the trash across the room near my work desk and pulls up his pants.

"We're all adults here. And friends might be stretching it with Law. We sort of work together and we had dinner. *Once.*

There's no bro code against fucking around with you when I met you first."

"It's not that." Now his shirt's back on, dammit.

"Then what is it?"

"It's hard to explain." One shoe on, one to go, and then he'll be gone for good.

"Anders ... it's okay."

"I gotta go. Thanks for, uh ..."

"Do you always thank your hook-ups for orgasms?" I ask. "I don't think I've met a more polite fuck buddy."

"We're not fuck buddies," Anders says. "It was a moment of weakness, and it's still not a good idea for me to be with anyone."

It's hard to hold in my eye roll. "It's just sex."

He winces. "I know. I didn't mean for it to sound anything more than that, but right now, just sex is too much for me to handle."

I purse my lips. "Are you okay? Like, really okay? I'm not asking because social conventions dictate I should—I really want to know. We don't know each other well, and Law may've mentioned something that screwed you up."

He glares at me.

"He didn't give me details, but if you need to talk or whatever ... I may not be relationship material, but my ears work. I'm a pretty decent friend, and I'm not saying that to get in your pants again. If you say you don't want sex, I'm cool with that."

Anders sighs and murmurs, "Thanks. I'll keep that in mind. But I should go."

"All right. I'd walk you out, but I don't think I trust my

legs at this point." The word spent doesn't begin to describe how sated I am right now.

The only thing ruining my after-sex glow is the fact he's rushing out of here like what we did was wrong.

The smile Anders gives me is almost cocky but not quite pulling it off. "I'm sorry. It's got nothing to do with you."

"Of course, it doesn't. I'm fucking awesome."

He chuckles. "God, you sound just like my brother."

"I'm seeing Law in a few days. If you want me to pretend this never happened, I can. Just let me know in case he asks."

"You think he'd ask?"

I shrug. "I don't know. I don't know him well enough to know how invested he is in your life."

"I would say pretty invested, but not *that* invested. In fact, when I talk about my sex life, he either leaves the room, tunes me out, or, in some cases, he covers his ears and sings 'Bohemian Rhapsody' really loudly—the opera part too."

I laugh. "Is he any good?"

"As tone deaf as a fish."

"How do you know fish are tone deaf?"

"They live underwater. You think they can hear music?"

We smile at each other, probably at the randomness of our conversation. Add in my state of undress and his freak out, and it makes for a really weird hook-up.

"I'll see ya 'round," Anders says and heads for my door.

"Thanks for the orgasm!" I call out.

It comes a bit late, but his laugh echoes through the apartment, right before the door shuts with a resounding click.

"*D*avis, if I have to tell you one more time to sit your a—butt—in that seat, I'm going to throw you out the bus window."

The other teachers had a right to warn me about him. He's disruptive, he's loud, and he'll do nearly anything to get attention. They don't see what I see though. It's not a cry for attention or a call for help. Davis protects himself the only way he knows how—by turning everything into a joke. I've seen it before. Hell, I've lived it. Ask anyone I went to high school with, and they'll tell you I was the class clown.

"Mr. Garvey is violent," Davis exclaims.

"It's not like you could actually fit through the bus windows," I mutter. "It's a minibus, for crying out loud."

The kids laugh, but it's not at the expense of Davis. This is only our second time heading for Law's dojo, but I already know this group is different with each other than they are during classes and around the rest of the students.

I haven't been nervous or weird about seeing Law after Anders' quick exit last week, but I don't realise there's a need to be until I walk in the shopfront doors and Law can't even look at me. His neck and ears are red, and if I had to guess, I'd say his beard-covered cheeks were burning too.

"Hi," I say.

Law lifts his head and grins. Oh, yeah, his brother has a big mouth. "What's up?"

"Really? *What's up*? You hang around teenagers way too much. You're starting to talk like them."

"Pfft," Davis scoffs behind me. "Dude, no one says *what's up* anymore. How old are you guys?"

"How old are you?" Law asks. "*Dude*? That was cool when I was in high school."

"You say dude all the time!" Davis exclaims.

"Whatever, dude. All of you go get warmed up." Law tilts his head in the direction of the bamboo curtain.

I go to follow them, but Law stops me. "I got you something."

"That sounds ominous."

He goes behind the counter and pulls out white clothes.

"A karate uniform?" I ask.

"It's called a gi, noob. Suit up, and I'll see you in there for all the mocking you can handle."

"You did this purely for your entertainment, didn't you?"

His laugh as he leaves the room sends a shiver through me. It sounds exactly like Anders.

I've left Anders alone since his desperate escape from my apartment, and I tell myself I only keep thinking about him because the sex was amazing. I might have trust issues bigger than Kanye West's ego, but fuck, I miss sex.

And it's best if I keep my distance from Law's brother, because even though I know they're identical twins and they're separate people, it's hard for me to differentiate between the two. Like just now when he laughed.

When I join everyone in the class, there's only minor ribbing about being a white belt when all the kids are at least a yellow belt. In my defence, they've been doing this six months longer than I have.

Towards the end of the lesson when Law trains the kids one on one, he turns to me. "Who wants to see if Mr. Garvey can get me on the ground?"

The kids hoot and holler, but I'm more worried about

sprouting wood at pinning my hook-up look-a-like to the mats.

I needn't worry though, because Law is one tall and sturdy fucker. I may be slightly wider, thanks to weight training at the gym, but it's obvious weights mean shit all in a hand-to-hand combat situation. After basic manoeuvres that don't work, I practically climb his back like a tree and still can't get him to budge. The kids laugh at me wrapped around Law, clinging onto him like a bloody koala.

With a quick grab of my wrist and a flick, Law has me over his shoulder and landing on my back with a thud.

I breathe hard, I'm sweaty, and my vision blurs as Law appears above me with a wide smile on his face.

"Chantel, wanna show him how it's done?" Law asks.

When he reaches a hand out to help me up, I pull him close and mutter so only he can hear, "You think this is a good way for me to earn their respect?"

He smiles and playfully pats my cheek a little too hard. "Nope, but it is a good way to give this shy girl some confidence. Sorry, I had to sacrifice you for the greater good."

I'm left speechless as I make my way to the water cooler for something to drink. It's obvious Law's passion for this runs deeper than he lets on. He says he started this because of something that happened to his brother, but he has a glimmer in his eye when one of his students *gets* it.

Chantel gets Law on the ground first try this time, and I think I'm even prouder of her than he is.

When the class ends and the kids file out to the front, I want to ask Law to go to dinner again tonight to talk more about teaching and his classes. I'm in awe of him, and if I become half the teacher he is, I'll be happy. Before I can embarrassingly fanboy over his teaching method, Davis approaches him.

The kid looks behind him to make sure none of the other kids are listening. "Hey, umm ... can I ask you something?"

"Sure."

I should give them privacy, but I've been explicitly told not to leave a student one on one with any other faculty—including contractors and substitute teachers. It might be overkill, and the school doesn't think Law would be a danger, but it's to protect us as much as it is the students. Pretty sucky world we live in to have these procedures in place.

"Is your brother going to come visit again?" Davis asks.

"I usually only invite him for the last week of school. He has to give notice to take time off work to come talk to you guys." Law glances at me and then back at Davis. "Why's that?"

Davis looks down at his feet. "No reason. It's all good."

"If you have anything you want to talk about, I'm always willing to listen. I have a good ear. Just ask Mr. Garvey. He whined all last week about how much of a handful you shitheads are." Law winks at me, knowing I'm listening in.

Davis cracks a smile. "Thanks. I'll ... uh ... keep it in mind. But this is something way out of your straight league."

I step forward. "I know I should pretend I didn't hear any of that, but, Davis, if you need someone to talk to who's"—I use air quotes—"*in the same league* as you, I have a good ear too."

"I'm good. It's nothing." Davis leaves before either of us can stop him.

I don't get a chance to ask Law about dinner, because my feet carry me into the reception area, chasing after Davis. I can't pull him aside though, because the room is now filled with little five-year-olds, parents, and my ten teenagers.

"Okay, my lot. File out to the bus."

I don't get a chance to talk to Davis when I drop them back at school either, because they all disperse into the parking lot where their parents await.

Davis's mum greets him with a warm smile, and granted I've witnessed a whole two-second exchange between them, but her welcoming doesn't indicate Davis has a problem at home. Maybe he wants to talk to Anders about something that's happening at school. Or maybe I'm overreacting and reading into it too much. But the point of me taking over the LGBTQ union was in hopes of getting these kids to open up to me. I want to create a support system so they don't have to go through the same shit I did when I was in school. The comments, the slurs … none of them were directed at me because I was closeted, but that doesn't mean they didn't get to me. My bullies were talking about me, even if they didn't know they were.

After returning the bus keys to the office, changing out of my gi, and grading some homework in my classroom, I find myself in my car, driving back to Law's dojo.

Something doesn't sit right with me about Davis, and I want to talk to Law and see what he thinks I should do. Forcing Davis into talking could push him away, and if it's something serious, I don't want to do that.

Law's locking up as I pull up in an empty parking spot out front. "Come back for another ass kicking?" he calls out. I go to get out of the car, but he opens the passenger side door and climbs in. "Thanks for the ride."

"I'm giving you a ride?"

"Sure. You want to talk about the kid, and I don't want to walk home. It's a win-win. I was expecting you. I saw the way you looked at Davis. You're worried."

"You a mind reader now? How do you know I didn't come here to talk about your brother?"

"Why would we want to talk about him for?"

My eyes widen. "Oh, shit. I thought he told you … or, I dunno, maybe I'm being paranoid—"

Law breaks into a laugh. "I know you hooked up again."

"You're an asshole."

"Only to my friends, and apparently, you're desperate for some of those."

"Well, when you're so kind …"

"So, the kid," Law says. "I have no idea what that was about this afternoon, but I can hazard a few guesses. If he wanted to talk to Anders, it has to do with the whole being a gay teen in a shitty world."

"The world isn't completely shitty anymore."

"Feels shitty to me," he mumbles.

"I was in high school only five years ago, and we never had student unions or any programs in schools to teach about LGBTQ issues. Now, I have ten students in my union alone. In *high school*. It's still far from perfect, but it's something. I'm worried why Davis couldn't come to me."

"Maybe it's that you're new. Maybe he doesn't trust you yet, or maybe it's because he knows he won't have to look

Anders in the eye every day after he gets whatever it is off his chest."

"How does Davis even know Anders?" I ask.

"Last term, Anders had a week off from work, so I told him he should come by the dojo and talk to the kids. They loved seeing us fight."

"Anders knows martial arts?"

"Do you guys talk at all?" he asks with a small smile. I think he already knows the answer to that, but I get defensive anyway.

"He told me you're a terrible singer." Yeah, we talk about the real intimate stuff.

"Well, we're identical so it takes one to know one. We both did martial arts training as kids, but he gave it up in high school. I think he realised how good I was and knew he couldn't compete, so it became my thing. He only recently came back to it. He told the kids his life story—which isn't a pretty one—so Davis probably thinks he'd understand what he's going through the most. Or we could be totally overreacting and he wants to ask Anders out. I think he developed a crush."

"He's fifteen! Anders is ol—"

"Watch it with the old shit," he warns. "And I'm not saying Anders would go for it—duh. He likes them young but at least legal."

My face falls. "Anders likes young guys? How young?" Why does that thought irritate me?

Law looks away. "I told you that you weren't his usual type. His normal hook-ups are eighteen and pretty."

"Are you saying I'm not pretty?"

He laughs. "No. You're all man." He lowers his voice

and I swear I hear him mumble "And hot," but I don't know any straight guys who call other men hot. "So what do you want to do about the kid?"

"I was hoping you had answers."

"Well, then we're fucked. I guess I could ask Anders to come talk to him …" If Law's tight expression is anything to go by, I'd say that's the last thing he wants.

"Can I ask you something about Anders? I know we said we wouldn't talk about him, and I don't want you to think I'm friends with you to get to him. We're just hooking up, and he swears it won't happen again … but he said that the first time, and—"

"Spit it out, Reed."

"Is he okay? Like … this whole cryptic something happened to him and he has a shitty story, and when he's with me, he seems jittery afterwards like what we did was wrong …"

"He's fine. He won't gut you in your sleep if that's what you're worried about. He's not psychotic."

"That's not actually what I was worried about. I'm worried about him in general. If it's something like an attack or bashing, it definitely explains his anxiety around intimacy."

"You think Anders' issues are from a hate crime?"

"Well you're both so fucking vague. What else am I supposed to think?"

"His problems are a lot closer to home," he murmurs. "Look, it's not my thing to tell, and you don't have to worry about it. Just know that it's nothing too serious and I handle it for him."

"Do you two have that weird twin voodoo where you

can sense the other at all times and know if something's wrong?"

"That's not a real thing. If it was, Anders wouldn't have issues."

I have no idea what he means by that, but I can't keep pushing. He's like a vault, and if I ever want to find out what happened to Anders, I'm going to have to earn his trust and hear it from Anders himself. If he ever contacts me again, which I doubt he will.

"Let's go get dinner," I say. "I'm hungry."

"Is this going to become a thing now? Monday night dinners with your only friend?"

I give him the finger. "As long as you keep giving me insider secrets on how to be a good teacher, I'll keep buying you dinner."

Law's hand lands on my shoulder. "You are a good teacher. I've seen it."

"Maybe with the union kids, but at school? Honestly, I don't know how much more I can take. I have this one class who keeps trying to dissect my sexuality. The union kids know but not the other students."

"What do you do in response?"

"At first, I told them to cut it out, but now I'm ignoring them, hoping they get over it."

"Ah, there's where you're going wrong. Like I said, treat them as adults. The school knows you're gay, right? They no doubt have an anti-discrimination protocol in place for when that gets out to the kids. If parents have an issue with a gay man teaching their children, you're protected by the fact everyone knows and administration is prepared. So, own up to it. Tell the kids you're gay and ask them if they have a problem with it."

"And when one of the smartasses says yes? I can't tell them to fuck off, can I?"

"No, but how would you handle that situation with an adult?"

"Tell them to fuck off."

Law laughs. "Okay, you're right. That won't work. In that case, tell them your sexuality has nothing to do with your ability to teach English. And if all else fails, do a monologue from *Dead Poets Society*. The kids will be all 'O Captain! My Captain!' before you know it."

"I have a confession to make. I know as an English teacher I should love *Dead Poets Society*, but …"

"It was the most boringest piece of shit in the history of movies?"

I nod. "And boringest is not a word."

"Sorry, teach."

I tense and whip 'round to stare at Law.

"Why are you staring at me weird?"

Other than the fact he sounded exactly like Anders when he called me that last week in bed, nothing at all. "Sometimes it's freaky how much you and Anders are alike."

"Identical twin, dude."

It doesn't feel that way though, and I don't know why. "Maybe it's a Clark Kent and Superman thing. I haven't seen you two together, so it's hard to believe you're two different people."

He rubs a palm down his thigh and shifts in his seat. "Umm … well—" He clears his throat.

God, I'm an ass. "I'm making you uncomfortable. Sorry. Forget I said anything. I want to be friends with you and hook up with your brother."

"Greedy much?"

"I don't want you to think I'm here for your brother or—"

"Reed, it's okay." His eyes pierce mine, and his mouth drops open to say something, but it dies along with his eye contact. He stares out the windshield as he asks, "We going to dinner or what?"

Even though Law says it's okay, he barely talks throughout our meal at the pub.

"I promise from now on I won't talk about your brother," I say after paying for the food.

"It's not that. I promise."

"Then what's up?"

He smirks. "*What's up*? Now who's been hanging out with teenagers too much?"

Classic avoidance tactic. I may not understand them, but there's no doubt I'm taken with both the Steele brothers. One on a professional and friendship level, and the other in a more biblical sense. I want Anders in my bed again, but with the way Law is reluctant and clamps up every time I mention his brother, I think it's best if I try to keep each of them separate for the time being. He's fine mentioning Anders on his own, but whenever I do it, he gets this weird look in his eye.

Keeping Anders under wraps won't be hard. I don't even know if he's going to come back for more.

8
LAWSON

*A*s soon as I get home, I add Reed on Facebook. Leaving the pub, he told me to add my phone number into his phone, but if I did that, he'd know I'm pretending to be Anders and he already has my number. So I gave him Anders' number and changed the last digit. I have no idea who Reed will reach if he ever calls or messages, but this way, he won't have to. He can private message me on Facebook instead.

The lengths I'm going to so he doesn't find out is getting out of hand. And I'm the one on Anders' case to get counselling. Ironic, really.

My phone dings with a notification.

Reed: Whoa, Facebook official? We really are friends now. I'm assuming this is Law, considering the impressive profile picture of your beard and the name "I Fought The Law." Tell me, did the law win?

THE shouldn't be capitalised by the way.

I grin.

I Fought The Law: Sorry, teach. Told you I suck at English.

PS The law kicked my ass.

Reed: No wonder I couldn't find either of you on Facebook. Is Anders' profile as cryptic as yours?

I Fought The Law: Stalking is illegal and creepy, you know.

Reed: You're illegal and creepy.

I Fought The Law: Careful, you sound like Davis.

Also, Anders doesn't have social media. He lives in the stone ages.

Reed: So the nineties?

I Fought The Law: Close enough.

Reed: Have you spoken to him about Davis yet?

I Fought The Law: He's out, but I will when he gets home.

If he gets home.

Can't really say that to Reed; though maybe I should. It might mean the definite end between the two of them, and I won't be tempted to do what I really want to do which is go over there and beg him to fuck me.

Ever since I met him, that's all I've thought about. Actually, that's not entirely true. After our first hook-up, I was willing to keep the memory and move on. It wasn't until he turned up at my dojo and I saw how he is with the kids and how much we have in common that I thought of wanting more. But I want more as me, not as my brother.

The fact we've had sex and he doesn't even know it kills me. I sat across from him and ate dinner, all the while knowing what he looks like naked, what sounds he makes when he comes, and how hot he is when he's trying to keep control but loses all restraint.

I want to tell him the truth, but I'll lose the chance to be with him and his friendship. Plus, we have to work together. There's no way of getting out of this without hurting him. The first time might've been forgivable had I come clean immediately. It was just a hook-up. But this last time was based on lies upon lies, and I'm not that guy. I'm not the asshole lying to get people into his bed. Usually.

The front door creaks open, and an exhausted Anders ambles through it with a scowl on his face.

"Bad night?" I ask.

"Was going all right until Kale turned up and threw a tantrum."

"The guy I broke up with for you a few weeks ago?" I jump up from my spot on the couch and follow him into our small kitchen. "You okay?"

"Yeah, I think he's harmless. It's not like he followed me there. He was just as shocked to see me as I was him. And it worked out because Chris dumped me."

"Wait … you're still dating that guy?" Why'd he agree to go on a date with Reed if he was seeing Chris? He can barely handle *one* relationship. If you can call what Anders has relationships.

Anders shrugs. "We're casual. Well, were casual. Apparently, he doesn't like drama. Of all the guys I had potential of breaking up with on my own, and he beats me to it."

His smile gives away his relief that he didn't have to be the one to break up with Chris—or have me do it.

Anders dismissing the run-in with Kale this easily is a huge step. Normally, he'd go into panic mode and wouldn't leave the house for a few days, convinced the dude is a stalker.

"What happened with Kale?" I ask.

"He was there with someone else, but apparently I'm still an asshole. What did you say to him when you broke up with him?"

"Just that he was too young for me … uh, you."

"Eighteen is not that young."

"Sure, what's a decade between fucks?"

"What's up your ass?" Anders snaps.

Not Reed, thanks to you. "Nothing," I mumble but then I can't help myself, apparently. "I think I fucked up."

"How?" Anders grabs a bottle of water out of the fridge and takes a sip.

I lean against the bench. "You know how our teacher said the wrong name the first day of ninth grade, and I didn't correct her? I was Dawson for the entire school year—"

Anders snorts. "Man, that was so funny."

"She had to take attendance every day. Did she think the L on my name was pronounced as a D?"

He laughs. "Hi, I'm Dawson with an L."

"I didn't call her out the first time, and then it was way too late to correct her. This is like that, but with a hook-up."

Anders shrugs. "Easy. Just say, oh, by the way, my name's Lawson not Dawson."

It's not that easy, but getting into it with Anders isn't a good idea. He could accuse me of identity theft. Then there's the whole coming out to him thing which I'm not ready to do. I will eventually. Just not while I'm fucked up over a guy.

"Even after we've already slept together?" I ask.

"Didn't you say it was a hook-up? Just move on. Plenty of pussy in the cattery … or something like that."

"Fish in the sea?"

"Why would you compare women to fish? Isn't that offensive?"

"I know you have no experience with women, brother, but trust me when I say they aren't too keen on being referred to as pussy either."

Anders shrugs. "Okay, so the way I see it, you either move on or keep up with the lie until you're done having fun. Face it, Law, you're not long-term material. You haven't had a girlfriend for longer than a few months."

"Hey, Olivia, Kirsten, and Dani all lasted a year … almost."

"Barely. And when was your last girlfriend?"

"You know when my last girlfriend was," I say.

Understanding crosses his face. "Have your fun with what's-her-face and move on like you always do. You know what they say—if you're going to be bad, be good at it."

"You're saying I should take advantage until it blows up in my face."

"Exactly. Not like you're risking a broken heart." My brother has become a cynical bastard over the years. "Now, if you'll excuse me, I'm going to bed to get reacquainted with my hand. It's been a while since we hooked up."

"Dude, I didn't need to know that."

Anders shrugs and goes to his bedroom.

Knowing what he's doing behind his closed door makes me want to leave the apartment, and there's only one place I want to go. I shouldn't take my brother's stupid advice. It's come from *Anders*. Not to mention it's misguided because he doesn't know all the facts. Does that stop me from taking it? Nope.

Like he says, the damage has already been done. I've already let Reed think I was Anders twice.

I almost grab my keys off the bench to leave when I stare down at the clothes Reed saw me in a few hours ago.

Change first.

Again, I wait for the realisation and reality of what I'm doing to sink in. I'm changing my outfit so the guy I'm hooking up with doesn't know who I really am.

Where's the guilt? Where's the angel that's supposed to sit on my shoulder and warn me against doing morally wrong things?

He's probably bent over and getting rimmed by the devil.

Now there's a nice thought.

As I arrive at Reed's apartment and climb the steps to the second floor, there's a moment of hesitance. I shouldn't be here. It's wrong.

My cock twitches.

Dammit. Perhaps part of my turn-on is the wrongness of it.

Reed's smile fills my head, and I realise, no, the wrongness is the only reason I'm still standing on this side of the door and not inside his apartment stripping him out of his clothes. My attraction to Reed is all him—not just his golden hair and toned muscles, but everything about him. From the gentle way he deals with his students and how he wants to be a better teacher to the way he bossed me around in bed last time.

If anything, I deserve credit for holding out until tonight to come back.

But if I do this—if I knock on his door again—there's no turning back. It *will* blow up in my face eventually. It will make shit awkward, and we work together. It might only be for an hour once a week, but I'll still have to see him when it's over. I could end it now and stay his friend as Law, just hoping Reed never crosses paths with Anders, or I could say fuck it and have Reed while I can. I'm already gripping the edge, dangling over the rabbit hole. All I have to do is let go. Or climb out. One or the other.

This is the second time in a matter of weeks that I'm having a staring competition with Reed's door.

With a deep breath, I knock. And there Reed is, wearing the hottest smirk I've ever seen. Morality, right and wrong, and the angel that's too busy getting fucked by the devil all disappear.

The way Reed looks at me when I'm Anders has my pulse racing and my breathing shallow.

I grip Reed's shirt and pull him close. Not a single word is spoken before our mouths meet and we make our stumbling journey past the kitchen and living room towards the back of his apartment to his bed. I read somewhere once that if you do something three times in a row it's classed as a routine. Each time I've been in Reed's apartment, we've fumbled our way around, too busy wrapped in each other to care about running into furniture.

"What do you want?" Reed asks and moves his lips to my neck. His hands reach under my shirt and press into my abs.

"I want …" I almost choke on the words. "I want you to …" What I really want is not to be nervous as fuck right now.

"Want me to fuck you?" he whispers.

I jolt away from him and take a few steps back.

"What's wrong? I thought—like, it's cool if you're not into that. What we did last week was fine by me." He reaches back and pulls off his shirt.

There's so much I want to do to him and him to me. The two times I've been with Reed haven't been enough, and I doubt this time will be either, but I need to treat every time like it'll be the last, because I'm hoping I come to my senses soon.

But not tonight. No fucking way.

"Anders?" Reed snaps me out of my hesitance.

"Sorry. Thinking. Umm, I want you to fuck me." My voice cracks halfway through, dammit.

"Are you sure about that? Why do I feel like you're about to say 'but'?"

"Confession time." I run my hand over my hair and grip tight, practically pulling it out from the roots. "I don't bottom. Like, ever." Unfortunately for me, because of oversharing on Anders' part, I know this is a partial truth about my brother. He used to—a long time ago—but not anymore. He can no longer give up that type of control. I shouldn't know this, but I do, and it all weaves in with how I fucking got here, pretending to be someone I'm not.

"*Never?*" Reed asks.

"Why's that so hard to believe?"

He shrugs. "You don't seem very ... toppy."

"Thanks? I think?"

"Don't mean anything by it. You just seem easy-going and up for anything, like your brother. Most guys who are exclusive tops are controlling and—"

"Are you about to get stereotypical on me?"

"I said *most* guys. Stereotypes exist for a reason. I do want to ask why you haven't bottomed before and why you want to with me though."

I must pull a face or visibly pale because he quickly backpedals.

"But the look on your face tells me you don't want to share that information, and we're supposed to be no strings attached, so I'll shut my mouth. We don't need to get into it."

"The opportunity hasn't presented itself." Not a lie, but something Reed will probably see right through. That's me talking, not Anders. What supposed twenty-eight-year-old gay man hasn't had the opportunity? "I mean, guy wise. No one I've wanted to go there with."

"You don't even know me. Hell, I know your brother better than I know you at this point."

This is going downhill. "And he talks about you. It's as if I know you, and that's good enough for me." I reach out and pull him towards me, bending slightly at the knees. I've been hard since before I knocked on the door, and when I push against Reed, he groans. My head dips, my mouth going to his neck. He shudders under my warm breath on his skin.

"Wait—" He tries to pull back, but I wrap my arm around his back and don't let him.

"No. More. Talking."

"Just tell me one thing. This isn't about proving something or you think it's some cure for emotional shit that's going on that I don't want to deal with later, right?"

Granted, I don't know Reed well, but that seems really harsh coming from him.

"I'm not trying to be a dick," he says. "I just don't want this to come back and bite me in the ass."

Welcome to my world. "You should take me being comfortable around you as a good thing. I promise I won't become clingy or ask for a relationship or any of that other stuff you don't want. I just want you to fuck me."

"Enough of a reason for me." Reed's hands wander over my already flushed skin. "I'm going to make this so good for you."

"Promises, promises," I mock.

Reed's mouth is soft as it searches out mine. Neediness and urgency have been forgotten after my admission and have been replaced with a reassuring touch.

I want to tell him I don't need intimacy—I just want to be fucked—but there's no denying his mouth has special abilities. I could stand here and kiss him all fucking night. Hell, give me long enough, I'm fairly certain I could come from kissing him.

His mouth is rough around the edges and strong—powerful. I'm comfortable handing all control over to Reed, and I don't think I've had that with anyone before.

A strong hand trails down my stomach, cupping my cock

through my jeans. "Need to take the edge off first or are you good to go?"

"There's never taking an edge off with you. Both times I've gone home thoroughly spent."

His grin lights me up inside, and I have to remind myself of why I'm here. This is just sex. Reed's not my friend right now or my colleague. He's not the guy whose smiles make me weak. He can't be that guy, because whatever this is between us has no future.

"You might not need it, but I do," Reed says. "I won't last two seconds inside you otherwise. I'm good for a few rounds, I swear. You'd know that if you didn't run off so fast whenever you're here."

Ignoring his attempt at passive-aggressiveness, I sink to my knees instead. "Let me take care of you first."

"Not gonna say no to that. Like ever."

My hands pause on his belt buckle, because his words sound different this time—like a promise of a future.

"What's wrong?" he asks.

"Nothing," I lie. "Just thinking about sucking you off until you come in my mouth."

"No more thinking. Just do it already."

As easy as that, the tension snaps and it's playful again. Instead of hurrying up though, I slowly kiss his hard abs while I tortuously undo his pants. When he grunts in frustration, I chuckle.

"You're an ass."

My hand wraps around his shaft. "Am I?"

Throwing his head back, Reed shudders. "Nope. You're awesome."

"Flattery will get you everywhere."

When his cock springs free of his boxers, precum leaks from the tip. I can't stop myself from tasting and lick across his slit. He mutters something unintelligible, but when I engulf him to the root and lightly suck, he goes completely silent minus some heavy breathing.

I work him over annoyingly slow with just enough firmness to drive him crazy. When he tries to thrust into my mouth, I grip his hip. If he whines, I go slower.

"I guess you're taking charge this time," he grinds out.

"Mmhmm," I moan around his cock.

"Fuck, Anders, you're killing me."

Whoosh. My brother's name works better than a bucket of ice water, but I don't stop. I couldn't force myself to even if I wanted to. My erection might be fading, but Reed is still hard and long, and so Goddamn good.

My hands wander up Reed's thighs and grip his ass cheeks hard. His cock nudges the back of my throat, and with my hands holding him in place, he's forced to do short and shallow thrusts.

I know he's close when he grips my hair, and I'm eager for it.

"I'm close," he pants. "If you don't want it, better move away." Unintelligible things fall from his mouth as the first spurts hit my tongue.

I suck him harder, swallowing his cum as he tries to mute a shout. I stay with him until he stops thrusting and pulls out of my mouth.

"Holy shit." Reed flops backwards onto the bed. "Give me a sec."

I stand and start stripping off my clothes. Slowly, I climb

his body and straddle him, my cock digging into his stomach.

"Mmm," he moans when I bring my lips to his. A strong hand trails down my back and grips my ass. His cock twitches beneath me.

"Fuck, you really are a horndog, aren't you?"

"Only for you, baby." Reed's eyes fly open. When his mouth drops open to backtrack, I cut him off by kissing him again. Long and hard. I don't want him to say it was a slip, even though we both know it was.

I suck on his tongue, and he grunts.

"Lube. Bedside table."

I stretch and reach for the drawer but falter when Reed's lips land on my pecs. He licks around my nipple and then gently bites down.

"Fuck," I hiss.

He takes the lube out of my hands and lathers it on his fingers. "We'll take it slow."

Even though nearly everything I've read on the internet about anal says the most important thing is prepping, I just want to get it over with and get to the good part.

When I nod, Reed cups the back of my head with one hand, as his fingers trail down my back.

"You set the pace, okay?" he whispers.

When a lubed finger breaches my hole, I tense for that moment of awkwardness I've experienced when doing this to myself.

Reed is patient with me as I get used to the uncomfortable feeling between my ass cheeks. There's pleasure mixed with a slight burn, and I know it'll get better once I relax—it's just getting my body to do it that's the issue.

With his free hand, Reed reaches between us. His cock is half-hard, resting against mine, but Reed grasps us both. As he slowly strokes us together, my hips involuntarily begin to move. His finger sinks deeper with each small thrust, and the friction on my cock makes my mind drift away from what's happening in my ass.

"You going okay?" Reed breathes.

My hand trembles as I lean on one elbow and brush his blond hair across his forehead. "More than okay."

When he adds a second finger, and I adjust, everything changes. I end up rutting against him in a frantic need for more. If I'm not careful, I could come like this—with him stroking my dick while I ride his fingers. The fullness in my ass and his tight grip on my cock has me seeing stars.

I grunt while Reed whispers small encouragements. My enthusiasm stirs his own dick into action, and before I know it, he's harder than I am as I move against him.

"Do you think you can take more?"

I freeze on top of him, the nerves suddenly too much. This feels amazing, but Reed's a lot bigger than his fingers.

"Did you want to come like this?" he asks. "We don't have to take it further tonight."

"I want to, but …" Yep, I'm chickening out. Motherfucker.

"Hey, it's okay. I don't want to do anything you're not ready for. I'm only asking because a few more minutes of this, I'm going to come again, and I want to know if I need to pull back."

The fact he gets so worked up over me turns me on more than I ever thought possible. Sex has always been better when it involved anyone other than my hand—that's a given. I enjoyed it, I got off on it, but with Reed, it's more than getting off. I want to come but make it last as long as possible at the same time. I don't want to reach the finish line, but I'm desperate for it. I'm desperate for him. For everything. Not taking it further tonight leaves a promise that I'll be back.

"Come," I encourage him. "Please."

When Reed's fingers move inside me, they hit that spot, and I'm suddenly lost to my own pleasure.

My eyes roll back, and my hips pick up their pace again, rocking against Reed. Our cocks, slick and leaking precum, slide easily against one another. Our breathing becomes ragged and loud to the point I don't know which sound comes from who.

It's sensory overload, and I grit my teeth as I come. Reed's hips buck upwards once, then twice, and then more warmth hits my stomach as he stills.

Neither of us moves for the longest time, our breaths mingling, limbs tangled. We're a sweaty, breathy heap of useless muscles right now.

When Reed finally pulls his fingers out of me, I wince at the loss—that connection—but when he raises his head to kiss me, I'm too distracted by his domineering mouth and commanding tongue to care.

He moans and grips my ass. "Please don't run off right now."

The sudden crash of reality doesn't take too long to happen after coming. I don't want to run off, but I have to. The more time I spend with him as Anders, the more chance I have of saying something I shouldn't. I try to pull out of Reed's arms, but he holds me tighter.

"At least stay for a shower to clean up first."

"A shower I can do."

Disappointment clouds Reed's eyes, but he nods. Not for the first time, guilt over lying to him almost makes me confess everything, but I can't. Not now. I'm too far gone. We've passed the point of being able to come back from this.

9

REED

"Mr. Garvey, do you have a boyfriend?" Keira asks from the front row of my classroom.

Here we go. *Again.*

I sit against the edge of my desk and give her eye contact as I try to address this my way one more time. "What does my private life have to do with learning English?"

"Umm ... nothing?" she squeaks.

"Have you asked Mrs. Sutherton if she has a boyfriend? Or Mr. Hill?"

"Eww, they're old," Todd pipes in.

"Old people deserve love too," I say. "So does anyone who's lesbian, gay, bi, trans, queer, gender fluid, pansexual—"

"Okay, I get it," Keira says. "I was just curious, because you always avoid talking about it. Only someone hiding something acts sketchy, sir."

I take a deep breath and relent, trying it Law's way. "I still don't know what the importance of it is when I'm here to teach you guys about writing and understanding poetry, or correcting your horrendous grammar, but no, I don't have a boyfriend."

Even if what Anders and I have seems a hell of a lot more than just fucking after last night. He almost gave me something that proves he trusts me, that maybe he could want more eventually, but then he chickened out. I have to remind myself he's not my boyfriend, and we were clear from the beginning that it's not what either of us want. Not to mention he still keeps running off as soon as we're done. It's also confusing as fuck when I see Anders and think of Law.

Don't go there.

My class is still staring at me, awaiting elaboration.

"But I will have a boyfriend one day. Does anyone have a problem with that?" My heart stops beating. I'm dead inside. I hope my face doesn't give away how vulnerable I am standing up here, waiting to be judged.

The silence hangs in the air a bit too long, and I think I get out of the worst of it when a voice travels from the back of the classroom.

"The only problem I have," Colleen says, "is you're too hot to be single, sir. Gay guys must be dumb."

I'm thankful the whole class laughs, because fuck, how am I supposed to respond to that?

"I *think* I'm flattered, Colleen, but I can assure you gay guys aren't dumb. Which is why I'm standing up here trying to teach you about Shakespeare."

"Ugh," Todd says, "another old person."

"I'll tell Mr. Hill you think he's as old as Shakespeare, Todd. I hear the sweet sound of detention."

The other kids laugh, but Todd doesn't appear impressed.

When the bell rings to signal my next class, I wait for muttered comments under breaths, evil looks, or plain snorts of disgust, but surprisingly, I get none of that. Now that I've taken the fun away from them, they don't give a shit who I am or am not dating.

When they've all left the classroom, I dig my phone out of my desk and send Law a message on Facebook.

Reed: *I love you.*

I Fought The Law: *Wrong brother, dude.*

Reed: *Shut up. Seriously. I just came out to my nosey class, and they didn't even bat an eye.*

I Fought The Law: *Respect.*

Reed: *Dinner tonight? To celebrate.*

I Fought The Law: *Twice in one week? I'm like your master. Teacher overlord extraordinaire.*

Reed: *Do you want a free meal or not?*

I Fought The Law: *I'm in. But it's my shout this time. This friendship thing goes both ways.*

Something churns in my gut, and though I have an inkling of what it is, I'm nowhere near ready to acknowledge it. The fact I had something great happen and the first person I thought to contact was Law and not Anders doesn't sit well with me. Yes, Anders and I are casual. And yes, he turns up on my doorstep, we fool around and have sex, and then he leaves before either of us have come down from the high properly, but shouldn't he be the one I first think of? He's the gay one. He's the one who'd celebrate my coming out more so than Law.

I tell my mind that Law was the right person because

he's the one who's been giving me advice on how to handle the situation. Looking forward to dinner tonight doesn't mean anything. Law is my friend.

Is that why when you were finger-fucking Anders last night you wondered what it would be like if he were Law?

Fuck, conscience, don't start with that. Please.

When I turn up a few minutes early to pick up Law, there's a lanky figure standing in the dark, shuffling from one foot to the other.

It's not until I pull into the carpark that I realise it's Davis. His hand fists at his side and then relaxes again in a repetitive motion, and he hasn't noticed me in the parking spot a few feet away from him.

"Davis?" I ask and climb out of my car.

He flinches and turns towards me, exposing the shiner on the right side of his face.

"What happened?" I rush to get to him, but he flinches when I get close, so I pause.

His bottom lip trembles. "N-nothing, Mr. Garvey. I … Nothing at all." He shoves his hands in his pockets and refuses to look at me.

"Whatever it is, I can help. I can—"

"I shouldn't have come here. I'm sorry. I have to go."

"Davis!" I call out after him as he runs down the street.

I run my hands through my hair, and the dojo starts emptying of Law's last class.

"Hey, you're early," Law says from the open doorway.

"Can you lock up fast? Davis was here, he has a black eye, and as soon as he saw me, he ran. He might've been coming to talk to you or look for Anders, and I think I've just fucked it up."

"Give me thirty seconds. He can't get far on foot."

He's twenty seconds according to my watch, but it feels like five minutes later when he reappears, still wearing his karate pants. He's at least managed to change into a dark T-shirt.

"He ran off that way"—I point—"so keep your eyes open." I drive at a crawl, but my heart beats frantically and I begin to sweat. What the hell is Davis involved in? Did the kids at school do it or someone else? Questions and scenarios fill my head, so much so I can barely concentrate on driving.

"Pull up over here," Law says. The sun's almost completely set, but it's bright enough to make out a darkened figure moving at a quick pace through a park entrance on the side of the street.

On foot, we follow Davis and find him sitting on a park bench, his head in his hands and quiet sobs echoing around the empty space.

"I'll stay back here. I spooked him before," I say.

Law approaches, and I stand close enough to hear but not scare Davis off.

"Davis?" Law takes the seat next to him.

Davis's head shoots up. "Law?" he croaks.

"You need to tell me what happened, bud."

"I …" His eyes find mine. "I can't. Not with *him* here."

My immediate reaction is to ask what the fuck I ever did to him, but Law's head is screwed on tighter than mine right now.

"Is it because you're worried he'll tell the school?"

Davis nods.

I step forward. "Davis, I won't say anything you don't

want me to. I want you to trust that you can come to me with anything, and I won't betray your confidence. Who hit you? Was it another student?"

Davis shakes his head. "My …" He sniffs. "My dad."

Law and I both tense. I literally just told Davis I wouldn't betray his trust, but he was right in not wanting to tell me. If a teacher knows or suspects violence in the home, we legally have to report it.

"Has this happened before?" Law asks.

Davis shakes his head again. His body trembles, and I don't know if he's cold or in shock. "You know how I asked to talk to Anders?"

"Yeah," Law says, dragging the word out.

"I'm not out to my parents. I … I wanted to ask him advice on how to do it, but it all became moot today anyway when Dad caught me kissing"—Davis looks at me and rephrases—"a guy in my room. Dad was supposed to be at work, and—"

"If you're not out, how are you in the LGBTQ student union?" I ask. "You needed a signed permission form from your parents to join."

Davis's mouth drops open. "I … umm …"

"You're not in trouble," I reassure him. I want to know how much trouble the school will be in if he was never supposed to be in my union.

"My mum signed it. You know how Chantel's straight?"

I did not know that, but I also don't know what that has to do with anything.

"She joined as an ally. Honestly, I think it's because she doesn't have any friends, but—"

"Davis, get to the point," Law says.

"I lied. I told my mum I was joining as an ally too. Claimed to want a better world and all that shit. She eyed me as if she didn't believe me and warned me not to tell Dad, but she signed it."

"Did he only hit your face?" Law asks.

Davis stares at the ground.

"Did he hit your boyfriend too?" I ask.

"No. He's not my boyfriend. But anyway, he ran home as soon as Dad called us fagg—"

"Don't need to repeat what he called you," I say, because I'm two seconds away from getting as riled up as Law. He's trying to hide it, but anger radiates off him.

"Did he only hit your face?" Law asks again.

Slowly, Davis rises from the bench and lifts his shirt. It's hard to tell under the darkening sky, but red skin marks his side.

"What in the ever-loving fuck?" Law yells. He shoots out of his seat and heads towards the park exit.

"It's not as bad as it looks," Davis calls after him.

Shit, what do I do? Stay with Davis or run after Law … "Lawson! Don't do anything stupid."

He ignores me and pushes his powerful legs harder.

"He's not going where I think he's going, right?" Davis asks, his voice small.

"Have you given the dojo your address? Or on any of the forms you had to fill out to go there?"

"I-I don't think so."

Okay, so he can't go and commit an assault. That's a good thing. "He's probably gone to cool off." I *hope* that's what he's doing. "Those are some serious injuries, Davis. You might have broken ribs or—"

"Honestly, it looks worse than it is. It barely even hurts."

"We should take you to the hospital to be sure."

"No." He flinches back.

"You have to report this."

Davis's face pales. "You said you wouldn't. You can't make me."

"And what's your plan? Go back home where he could do it again? You came to the dojo because you have nowhere else to go. Why didn't you go to your boyfriend's—uh, non-boyfriend-make-out-buddy's house?"

"He's not out."

"I'm guessing he's not part of our union?"

"Can't be if he's closeted, can he?"

"You managed." Disappointment crushes me. This program is supposed to help students, but the loopholes are blaringly obvious right now. Davis had to lie to get permission to get into the program. This other kid isn't out, so he's not a part of it. It's great to have support when they need it, but when we make the kids jump through hoops to get it, of course not everyone is going to be on board.

Law reappears, still charging like a bull towards a matador. His head hangs low, and his hands are in his pockets. "I'm sorry I took off. I needed to calm down." His voice is flat and unemotional, but he's still agitated and riled up. He's just able to hide it better now. "You need to report this."

"And what? Have my dad arrested? Yeah, I'm sure he'll let me back in the house then."

"Where's your mum?" I ask.

"At work." Davis looks at his watch. "Although, she'll be home by now."

"And probably wondering where you are," I say. "We need to call her."

"We'll do it from the station because this is getting reported," Law says again.

"Law—" I start, but Davis cuts me off.

"I have nowhere else to go," Davis says. "If I report him—"

Law steps forward and puts his hand on Davis's shoulder. "I'll be with you the whole time. Most likely, your dad will be slapped with a domestic violence order and told to stay away from you. What about your mum? Do you think she feels the same way as your dad about you being gay?"

"I don't think so. I ... I don't know."

"Anything would be better than getting another black eye. You need to report it, Davis. You can't let this happen. You remember when Anders came to talk to you guys?"

Davis nods.

"Remember his story?"

Even I don't know Anders' story, but Davis does?

"That was different," Davis says.

"Not really. A person who was supposed to love him attacked him, and the only reason he got that chance was because Anders ignored the warning signs. This is a big-ass warning sign, and you need to stand up for yourself before your dad takes it one step further."

"He wouldn't ..." But Davis's words die, because we all know we've seen this story before. We've heard similar stories in the news and on social media.

"We can't take the chance," I say softly. "Will you come with us to the police station?"

"You ... you guys will be with me?"

"Of course," Law says.

"Every step of the way," I say. "And I know I said I wouldn't tell the school, but—"

"They're going to find out anyway because of the police report," Law says. "So when that happens, just know that Mr. Garvey had nothing to do with it. He's possibly one of the best guys I know, so you should have no trouble trusting him if you need someone."

Davis's gaze flits between us. "If I didn't know any better, I'd say you two were fuck—"

"Davis," I snap, but it's good to see he isn't completely lost to the events of tonight.

10

LAWSON

My hands itch to do something.
Punch someone.
Strangle Davis's dad.

I want to do what I should've done five years ago when I found Anders lying in a pool of his own blood.

Maybe that's why my hands are itchy. The creepy, dirty feeling is back. I'm covered in Anders' blood all over again, and it won't wash off. I'm in my own personal Macbeth hell.

Reed sits beside me as we wait for Davis to give his statement. Because neither of us is his legal guardian, we couldn't be present for the actual interview. They've called his mum, and she's apparently on her way, but that doesn't stop me from watching the clock, or my leg from bouncing.

A strong hand clamps down on my thigh. "He'll be okay," Reed says. "This is the right thing."

I don't tell Reed why I'm really freaking out. There are too many memories. Too much blood.

I shake that thought free. Davis is not Anders. Davis is not in a hospital bed fighting for his life.

"Law, what's wrong? You're shaking."

I can't look at Reed. I can't talk about it.

"We need some fresh air." Reed stands and brings me with him, hooking my arm in his and dragging me. My feet don't want to cooperate and almost trip over themselves.

When we reach the brick steps just outside the entrance, the cold snap brings me back into focus. I didn't grab a coat when I left the dojo, and even though Queensland winters aren't harsh, getting around in a T-shirt and thin pants isn't ideal. Reed changed back into normal civilian clothes before he came back to pick me up, so he doesn't have my issue. I shiver, and I can tell by the assessing way Reed looks at me that he's wondering if it's still part of my freak out or if I'm actually cold.

"It's cold." I don't think he believes me. I was running around the park less than an hour ago.

Even though he thinks I'm lying, he takes his jacket off and wraps it around my shoulders. "Okay, I think it's time you tell me what happened to Anders."

"Why?" I ask as I slip my arms into the holes. The sleeves only go to my wrists, but it's better than nothing. I'd feel bad about making Reed cold, but I think his agitation is doing a good job at keeping him warm.

"Because you look like you're about to faint, and you're the most casual person I know."

"I'm the only person you know," I mumble. I shove my hands in the warm pockets and avoid eye contact with Reed at all costs.

"Heard that. Sit." Reed practically pushes me down on a step. "Spill."

I go to open my mouth, but he cuts me off.

"You don't have to get specific, but I'm guessing it was a domestic abuse situation, right? Is that why you look like you're ready to hurl?"

Swallowing hard, I manage a small nod.

"Your father?"

I shake my head.

"Mother, uncle, aunt, what?"

"Boyfriend," I choke out.

Reed flinches. Yeah, no one really expects that. Anders is built like me. We're tall and lanky, but we're like ten percent body fat. The rest is muscle. But Kyle was twice Anders' size.

"An ex hurt him?"

That's an understatement. I always knew there was something off about the guy, but I figured he was just another person who couldn't handle that Anders and I were a package deal. Wouldn't have been the first time a girlfriend or boyfriend got jealous of us monopolising each other's time.

"He tried to kill him," I say.

"Fuck." Reed runs his hands through his hair. "Why didn't he tell me? Shouldn't he tell someone he's seeing about shit like that?"

God, this is a clusterfuck. He's not dating Anders. He's dating *me*. The truth wants to come out, but I have to swallow it down. I can't dump Anders' shit on him as well as my own. Not at once. "You're not dating, are you? You're fucking. That's what you keep telling him."

"I …" Reed shuts his mouth. "He should've told me. I asked him if … dammit, no, I promised you I'd never talk to you about your brother in this sense, so I'll leave it. He can explain it to me."

This is what I don't need right now. The stress of lying to Reed on top of sitting out here waiting for Davis is too fucking much. Davis was lucky to get away when he did. Who knows how far his father would've taken it. Visions of a faceless guy beating Davis to the point it's caused bruises … God, are my classes even doing anything at all to help these kids?

I sniff, and then I realise my cheeks are wet. Great, I'm fucking crying now.

"Shit." Reed's arm wraps around me and he pulls me to his side.

His touch is tender and warm, and even though this is the worst possible time to be turned on right now, my cock stirs.

Hell. Reed only needs to come near me and my body acts on its own accord.

"You know how you asked me if Anders and I have that twin thing where one can sense something's wrong?"

Reed nods.

"When he was attacked? There was nothing. He was complaining to me about something being not right. He'd tried to end it so many times, but Kyle kept coming back for more. I told him to suck it up, stay strong, and tell Kyle to fuck off. He did, but Kyle turned up the next morning asking for one last chance."

"It sounds like an abusive relationship just from his

actions. Not taking no for an answer, turning up uninvited …"

"I don't think he'd ever been physically violent with Anders before, but it was last chance after last chance with him. There were a lot of red flags in his behaviour that both Anders and I ignored. One time we went to a friend's party, and Kyle hated that I was hanging around them the whole night. Like he wanted to show off the fact Anders was there with him, as if Anders were a trophy."

It all seemed innocent enough. We chalked it down to Kyle being a little possessive, and I think Anders liked the whole being claimed by a caveman thing.

"If we'd known how fast it could escalate …"

"That's the thing with abusive relationships," Reed says. "You don't suspect your partner of so many years—someone who's supposed to understand you and protect you—to be the one who hurts you. Even with the signs, it's something you're blinded to until it actually happens and shows you the reality of how bad it's gotten."

Protectiveness I've only ever felt for Anders stiffens my spine. "You sound like you speak from experience." And if I'm not angry enough as it is, an urge to find out who hurt Reed and—

He sees the anger rising in me and puts his hand on my forearm to calm me. "No. My ex may be a selfish asshole, but he was never abusive. My sister had this thing with this guy in high school. I didn't understand it until I went to uni and took a semester of child psychology focusing on domestic relationships. It was more about learning to look for signs of abuse while teaching—like Davis asking for your brother last week."

"The day Anders was attacked … When I didn't hear from him, I assumed he chickened out." I let out a humourless laugh. "When my brother lay almost dying, I was in bed with my girlfriend, thinking Anders was a pussy for not breaking up with Kyle. Some twin connection, huh? I should've known, dammit."

"What happened to him wasn't your fault."

"You sound just like him. And his therapist." No matter how many times I hear it, I can't help feeling like I'm somewhat to blame. Not for Kyle's actions but for not taking it as serious as it was. When Anders didn't call, I should've known something was wrong with my brother.

Reed's brow furrows.

Thinking about this all again has the memories flashing through my brain on repeat. I lean forward and put my head in my hands. "I can't believe I'm back here again."

I'm sitting on the same stairs I walked up while having a police officer on each side of me. While Anders was at the hospital, I was here being interrogated as to why I'd want to kill my brother.

"They thought I did it," I whisper. "They thought I tried to kill my own fucking brother." I was stuck in an interrogation room for two hours before they realised they had the wrong guy. The whole time I sat there telling them it wasn't me, I took their hard questioning and believed I deserved it for not getting to Anders sooner.

"Please tell me they arrested the guy?" Reed asks.

I nod. "Kyle ended up turning himself in. Claims he lost it, it wouldn't happen again, blah, blah, blah. He only got a few years. He's eligible for parole next year."

"Shit." Surprising me, Reed brings me in for a hug and

forces my head down on his chest. I quietly sob, no longer caring about the whole being a grown-ass man bawling his eyes out.

A booming voice travels across the parking lot. "This is where he bloody gets it from."

Reed stands up so fast, I'm almost knocked off balance. "Mr. and Mrs. Sullivan."

Wait ... Davis Sullivan.

Motherfucker.

I stand too and lunge for the guy who put bruises on his fifteen-year-old kid, but Reed holds me back.

"You two faggots tell my boy it was okay to be like you?"

I push to get to him again, but Reed is strong for a guy two inches shorter than me. Granted, I could get out of his hold, but to do it, I'd have to hurt him, and I don't want to do that. My head swivels to meet Davis's mother's gaze, and she at least has the decency to hang her head in shame.

"You brought him here?" I hiss at her.

"The policeman on the phone said to bring him in if he'll come willingly; otherwise, they'd send a squad car." Her voice, so meek, gains absolutely no sympathy from me.

"If anyone should be arrested, it should be you two perverts."

Oh, for fuck's sake.

"I taught my son how to be a man today."

"By beating him?" Reed asks incredulously.

"Beating," the man scoffs. "It was a tap. A lesson. I barely touched the kid."

"Dan, stop," his wife begs.

"Why should I? Who are they to Davis anyway?"

"They're his teachers," she whispers.

"Does the school know they've got these perv—"

"If you call these gentlemen one more slanderous word …" Sergeant Boyd's words die along with his threat. We met with him when we brought Davis in, and he's one intimidating guy. He looks like an angry Dwayne Johnson. Boyd steps up beside Reed and me. "Are you Daniel Sullivan?"

Suddenly, the dickwad changes his tune. "I am. This is all one big misunderstanding, and—"

"Is that so? Because while you were too busy yelling at these men who brought your son in, you didn't notice me leave the premises or stand a few feet away from you when you said you, and I quote, 'Taught your son to be a man.' Would you care to explain how?"

"Where's my son?"

"Inside being interviewed."

"You can't do that," Mr. Sullivan says. "He's fifteen. You need a parent or guardian with him."

"I can assure you, sir, that when a complaint is made against said parent or guardian, the only person we need in the room with us is someone from the Department of Children's Services."

"This is getting out of hand," Davis's mum says. "He was angry. He didn't mean it."

"Yeah, because he seems so remorseful and accepting of gay people right now," Reed says and gestures to himself.

Sergeant Boyd turns to us. "You two are free to go whenever you want. I think this is going to be a long night."

Reed looks at me, but I shake my head. "All the same, we promised Davis we'd stay for him in case he needed us," he says.

"Wish the community had more teachers like you." The

sergeant turns to Mr. Sullivan. "Daniel Sullivan, you are being charged with assault and will be issued a domestic violence order. You'll be put in a holding cell until morning when you'll face a judge in family court. DOCS will decide if Davis is safe enough to be in the home tonight or will need to be given emergency accommodation if they believe there is still a threat."

"There's no threat," Davis's mum says, and I let out a relieved breath. Part of me was waiting for her to start with the slurs. "Not from me. I …" Her gaze flicks to her husband's, but she looks away as she says, "I already knew Davis was gay."

Thank God for small mercies.

"You knew?" Mr. Sullivan roars, and his wife flinches.

Sergeant Boyd reaches for his handcuffs. "Mr. Sullivan, don't make me use these."

Davis's asshole father puts his hands up in mock surrender and steps back. One minute he's yelling, and the next he's calm, and I begin to wonder if this is really the first time he's laid a hand on his son. His erratic behaviour reminds me of Anders' ex.

As the sergeant leads Davis's parents into the police station and they disappear, I almost wish for them to come back. Reed stares at me, as if assessing me or trying to figure me out. He's trying to see the ugly inside and realise why I'm on the verge of a breakdown right now.

"You still hungry?" he asks. "We're going to be here a while, so I can go for a walk and bring something back for us."

The thought of swallowing food makes my gut churn, but it'll be a distraction. It'll be good to get a break from

Reed for a few minutes to catch my breath and compose myself. "Yeah. I don't want to leave, but I could eat."

The reprieve is short-lived when Reed returns way too soon, and the food he brings tastes like cardboard as it goes down my throat. It doesn't sit well in my stomach either.

Waiting another hour for Davis doesn't help.

"You don't look well," Reed says.

An automatic playful *fuck you* is on the tip of my tongue, but I swallow it. "I'm fine."

"I can handle it from here. Maybe you should go home."

My hand fists on my bouncing leg. "I'm not going anywhere." I'm definitely not going home. God knows what Anders' reaction will be if he sees me like this.

"Do you want me to call Anders to come pick you up?" He grabs his phone of out his pocket, but before he can hit dial on *my* number, which is in *my* pocket, I snatch it out of his hand.

"Calling Anders is the last thing you should do right now."

"Why?"

"He has triggers, okay? This? This will be a major setback for him."

"What about for you?" Reed's hand goes to my thigh again, and this time when my leg stops bouncing, he doesn't remove it.

With one reassuring touch, I'm no longer covered in blood and guilt. I stare at his hand and wish I could cover it with mine, but I can't, and that makes me hate myself a little more. Reed notices my eyes glued to his hand, and he retreats.

"Sorry. I didn't mean anything by it. Just wanted your leg to stop bouncing."

I shake my head. "That wasn't … I mean, I know. It's cool." *Come clean. Tell him you want him as you and not Anders. Apologise profusely and promise to make it up to him.* "Reed, there's something—"

Reed stands as Davis and his mother appear.

Of course. Great timing.

They approach us with Sergeant Boyd, and Davis's mum is teary, her eyes red and watery.

"Here's my card," the sergeant says to Davis. "If anything happens, anything at all, you call me directly."

Davis avoids eye contact with his mother as he takes the card.

"Are you sure you're okay going home?" I ask.

Davis nods, but I glare at his mother.

"I didn't know." Her breath shudders. "The bruises. I wouldn't have …" She breaks down in a sob, and Davis throws his arms around her in comfort. "I didn't know how bad it was. I'm sorry."

"We're not the ones who need the apology, Mrs. Sullivan," Reed says.

With a single nod, she wraps her arm around her son's shoulder and leads him to the exit. I'm less anxious about Davis going home with her now, but the tightness in my chest refuses to leave as I watch them walk out the doors.

Reed's hand lands on my shoulder. "Come on, I'll take you home."

"I can't." The automatic response flies out of me.

"Why not?"

"I'll sleep in the dojo. I can't be at home in case …" *Stop. Talking.*

"In case what?"

I sigh. "I was the one who found Anders all those years ago, and after the attack, we both couldn't sleep. He dreamed of dying, and I dreamed of finding him dead. He'd turn up on my doorstep at two a.m. because he was still living where his boyfriend had tried to kill him. After that, we found a new place and moved in together, and we kept each other company at night. We usually both ended up on the couch watching TV. If I go home, I risk waking him, and I can't … I can't do it to him when he's made so much progress."

"Law, I'm going to ask this again, because you didn't seem to answer me before. You've always been there for Anders, but who's been there for you?"

Fuck, I'm on the verge of tears again, because the answer to that is no one. No one has been there for me. Counselling costs a shit ton of money, and our parents and I agreed that Anders' therapy was more important. To protect him, I essentially neglected my own demons, and after tonight they're back to haunt me. Thanks to a government-funded program, I got six sessions of counselling free after the attack, but it wasn't enough. That's clear now. If something like this has triggered me, what's going to happen the next time it occurs? I have to face facts that the likelihood of it happening again is high. Running a self-defence class for LGBTQ youth, I know for a fact Davis won't be my only student in need of help, because the world is that screwed up.

"Come home with me," Reed says. "I'll even let you take my bed. My couch is comfy enough."

I want to say yes. So fucking bad. But how am I supposed to keep my hands off him when we're in the Anders bubble I created inside Reed's apartment? "I can take the couch," I find myself saying even though I shouldn't.

"You're taller than me. You won't fit on my couch."

"I'm good with whatever. I just don't want to go home."

Anders is going to counselling again, and he's turning up for training sessions with me at the dojo. He has a life now. It's a bit manwhorey of a life, but that's better than holing himself in the apartment for days on end.

I won't fuck that up for him, even if it means screwing myself over even more. Digging a mighty big hole for myself, that's for sure.

11
REED

Law's pained voice has me scrambling off my couch so fast I almost hit my head on the coffee table as I try to find my feet.

"I'm sorry, I'm sorry, I'm so sorry," he chants. "My fault. I'm too late. Too late."

I cautiously approach the bed. "Law?"

"Anders." The anguish in his voice is heartbreaking.

"Hey." I drop to my knees beside the bed and try to wake him by cupping his rough jaw. "Lawson."

His body relaxes, and one of his eyes cracks open. He breaks out into an adorable half-smile.

No. Not adorable. The guy in your bed is not the guy who's usually in your bed.

Law leans towards me, and before my reflexes kick in—or my brain has time to register what he's doing—his lips are on mine.

What the fuck?

His mouth is warm and soft. It sends a shock straight to

my groin. Emotions I don't understand threaten to surface, but I push them back down.

I've never had a single moment in my life where everything clicked and fell into place. Never had that realisation that this is what I live for. But having Law's mouth on mine, his tongue teasing the seam of my lips, it's the first time I've ever craved that belonging sensation. Like I belong with him.

Fuck, this is so wrong.

"Law?" I murmur against his skin.

His eyes widen, and he pulls away. "Shit. I'm sorry."

"Do you often kiss people in your sleep?" I wipe my mouth but not because I didn't like it. I liked it too much. Way too much from a straight guy whose brother I'm screwing.

"More than you'd think." Law's head hits the pillow with a disappointed thud. "I was dreaming, wasn't I?"

"Think so. You don't remember what it was about?"

"No."

"You were calling out for your brother. And then you opened your eyes and kissed me. If I had dark hair, I'd probably worry you were trying to kiss Anders."

He laughs again, but there's no humour this time. "We may be fucked up, but we're not *that* fucked up."

"You're not fucked up at all, Law. You went through some messed-up shit, and you're allowed to have issues, but that doesn't mean you're irrevocably fucked up."

"Irrevocably," Law mumbles. "It's too middle of the night for big words, teach."

"Can I get you anything? Water? A shot of whisky?"

"Whisky will probably make it worse." Law sits up and

runs a hand over his tired face as he yawns. "I'm not getting back to sleep anytime soon. I may not remember what I was dreaming about, but I know I don't want to go back into it. I've had it a million times before. You want to take the bed and I'll watch your TV for a while?"

"I'm up now too. We can watch something together." I don't think leaving him alone right now is the best thing to do. I stand and then realise that's a bad idea when my cock tents in my boxers and pretty much lines up with Law's face. He sees it too, and instead of shock or embarrassment on his face, I swear his lips turn up into a smile. Before he can say anything, I clear my throat and turn on my heel.

"I don't need a babysitter," he calls after me.

I ignore him, not only because I think he's lying but also because I don't want to go back to sleep. After that kiss, I don't know if I'll be able to. I go back to the couch and sit at one end, covering my hard-on with my blanket. Law's lips were on mine for two bloody seconds, and my cock refuses to deflate because of it.

It's because he looks like Anders, I remind myself.

Yet, when he sits next to me, also only in his boxers and a T-shirt, and he stretches his long legs out, my dick gets harder, not softer.

I'm in trouble.

"Uh, umm," I stammer, "what do you want to watch?"

"Anything where I don't have to think."

"So anything made after 2001?" I flick through the Netflix selection and arrive on the first brainless one I come across.

"*The Hangover?*" Law asks.

"It's so far past ridiculous that it's funny."

"That'll work."

As the movie starts, I try to settle in next to Law on the couch, but all I can think about is his soft lips and the way he kissed me. It was brief but somehow needy, grateful, and hot at the same time.

"Okay," Law says, "marry, kill, fuck three of the actors in this movie. Go."

I smile. "That's easy. Marry Justin Bartha, fuck Bradley Cooper because he's Bradley-fucking-Cooper, and kill Zach Galifianakis because I'm pretty sure he'd be the same in real life as he is on screen."

Law narrows his eyes. "You came up with that answer way too easily. Makes me think you've thought hard about this in the past."

"How would you answer then?"

He bites his lip as if thinking about it. "Kill Ed Helms because his face and voice annoy me, fuck Bradley Cooper because I agree with you on that one, and marry Heather Graham."

He finds Bradley Cooper hot?

Don't read into it, my mind tells me. It's just a game. If given the chance to actually fuck Bradley Cooper, he wouldn't do it. He's straight.

But he did kiss me.

"Is Heather Graham your type of woman?" I manage to ask. "A stripper?"

Law lets out a laugh. "An actress playing a stripper, yes. I said actors, not characters. If we're going to marry a character in this movie, it'd have to be Justin Bartha's character too. He's the only one of them who isn't insane."

And a man …

I suddenly find myself extremely interested in Law's type. "What about real girlfriends? Have they been the insane type or the stripper type?"

"Sometimes both."

I can't tell if he's joking or not.

"Do you really want to know this stuff?" he asks.

I shrug. "It's three a.m. I'm just trying to stay awake for you."

"Go to sleep. I'll be fine."

"Now that you're not answering, it makes me more interested. What happened? Been cheated on? Lied to?"

He shakes his head. "No, nothing like that. I guess my problem is it always fizzles out. Like I get bored. I had two relationships that lasted about a year but knew a few months in it was never going to last. In the end, we decided we were better off as friends. But that didn't happen. Never saw either of them after that. The last relationship I had was the girl I was with when Anders was attacked. It was probably my worst breakup. She said the attack fucked us both up and she couldn't deal with Anders turning up at my apartment at all hours of the night. She said he was too dependent on me and basically asked me to choose between her and my brother."

"Whoa. And she called *you* fucked up?"

"It's a bit of a long story. I tried to make it work. Tried so hard to make both Anders and Olivia happy, but that was impossible. When I started staying at Anders' place, she thought I was cheating on her and neglecting her. She never said the words it's me or him, but that's the choice I had in the end. She left when I told her Anders was moving in with me."

"That's messed up, man."

"It's okay. It was better to find out when I did than if we'd gotten married or something. And again, I wasn't all that cut up about it ending. I dunno. I've never had that person. The *one*, or whatever you want to call it. I think it's a load of shit. The person you end up with is just a person you can tolerate for long periods of time."

I burst out laughing. "Yeah, but putting that into marriage vows isn't as poetic as saying it was meant to be."

Law lets out a less than dignified "Pfft."

I sigh. "I thought I had it once. Shit, I paid for the guy to fly to Europe to meet my sister, it was that serious. I had visions of a civil ceremony, little adopted babies running around everywhere … fuck, I was an idiot."

And I haven't really thought much about Ben since I moved to Carindale. Back home, his ghost wouldn't leave me alone. I'd lived with him, so even when he left me, his memory was still there. The small kitchen to my childhood home no longer haunted me with memories of Mum cooking us food and packing our school lunches but with Ben making coffee in his underwear with an adorable smile on his face.

I hate that smile now.

I had to get out of there. Unable to bring myself to sell the house, I rented it out, and the rent pays off the remaining mortgage for us. That, and Evie would kill me if I sold our house that was technically both of ours, even if prior to moving out, I was the only one contributing to the repayments.

I don't think I could live there again, even if I do move home eventually. Everywhere, I saw Ben and relived the heartache. The *confusion*. I wondered what I did wrong and what I could've done better. It took me a few months of thinking the problem was me before realising Ben was just a dick. What I saw in him, I'll never know. Heck, even my fuck buddy situation with Anders is healthier than what I had with Ben. That's saying something, because I still can't work out Anders' deal. Or my current deal with his brother.

"What happened?" Law asks.

I hesitate for a second, because I don't really want to get into it. But Law gave a big piece of himself tonight when he talked about what he and Anders went through, and that's a whole lot worse compared to my pathetic breakup. "It started out small. The lying. Like, he'd always say he had no money when it turns out he did. He made me pay for everything, while he saved up his money for a new car or a holiday he didn't invite me on. He said he was visiting his mother when he was going out with his friends and didn't want me to come."

"What the fuck?"

"When I confronted him, he blamed me. Said I was too smothering or whatever. Said I can't be alone and am clingy and thinks it has to do with my parents' death. After they died, my sister took off, and I'd been alone ever since. And then when I met Ben, I ... I guess I was scared he'd leave too."

Law's brow furrows. "That doesn't sound like you at all. I mean, the way you asked for us to be friends was a little weird—"

I laugh.

"—but I assumed it was because, as adults, it's hard to

make friends. It's easy as a kid. You walk up to someone, and bam, you're friends. You don't seem clingy to me at all."

"It's taken six months of being alone for me to realise Ben was just coming up with excuses for his shitty behaviour. I like having a boyfriend, and I want it all one day, but there's a difference between knowing what I want and being clingy. I want a boyfriend who actually wants to spend time with me."

"Wow, you're so demanding," Law says dryly.

"My issues with Ben had nothing to do with my parents and everything to do with the fact he just didn't want to settle down and wasn't man enough to tell me."

Law looks away. "In his defence, you're young. You shouldn't be thinking about settling down yet."

"I'm only four years younger than you and Anders."

"Do either of us look married?"

"Touché. Still, on my list of things I want to find, lying douches are on the bottom."

Law does that nervous twitch thing, and I begin to wonder if he knows something about Anders and isn't telling me. I can't ask because I promised him I wouldn't talk about his brother.

And when he goes back to watching the movie, I can't bring myself to dig for an answer. Mainly because I don't think I want to know.

I don't make it to the end of the movie before sleep pulls me under.

"Reed?" someone whispers in the dark.

I bury my head in my pillow but then realise it's hard. And not a pillow, but abs. Really nice abs.

"Anders?" I murmur and run my hand under his T-shirt.

Damn, this guy's body. All lean and hard. Wait … that doesn't make sense. Anders never stays over, and—"Fuck." I jump off the couch.

Law stays on the couch, blinking rapidly.

"Apparently I get molesty in my sleep," I say.

He laughs. "It's all good. We just fell asleep on the couch. No molesting happening here." When he stands, he stretches his long body and my eyes gravitate to the tent in his boxers. Then I have to turn away because, fuck. Fuckity fucking fuck. "Reed. Stop freaking out. I'm cool. But, uh … I should go." He dresses quickly while I continue to stand here like a moron, unable to say anything.

Then I realise I'm standing here with a hard-on, watching my fuck buddy's brother put pants on and wondering why I'm wishing he wasn't leaving.

I'm so screwed.

"Let me get this straight," Brody says with a laugh. "Or … not straight as it would seem."

I glare at my childhood friend over the candlelit dinner table. He picked this restaurant, claiming it's the best in the city. It's too upscale for my tastes. The murmurs from other tables are low and serious, and Brody's laughter bounces off the ceiling-high glass windows that overlook the marina. This is a serious restaurant, where everything is dignified. I feel out of place, like a kid sitting at the grown-ups' table. Especially with Brody laughing the way he is.

A waiter glares as he walks by, and I can't help wondering if he makes more money than I do.

"Laugh it up," I say to Brody. "This isn't my life or anything." I take a sip of the two-hundred-dollar red wine Brody ordered. It tastes like any other red wine. I'd make a terrible rich person.

Back when I knew Brody, it was all cheap beers his older brother could buy us and even cheaper cigarettes. Sitting in a fancy-ass restaurant while we sip on expensive wine—that he's totally going to pay for because who the fuck pays that much money for wine?—I can't believe this is where Brody Wallace ended up. My high school sweetheart. Or whatever. We weren't much of sweethearts but more each other's closeted fool-around friend.

We survived high school together. We let everyone believe we were best friends. We were way more than that, but there wasn't anything beneath surface level. With a few handjobs and blowjobs passed between us, it's not like we were serious. He's a great guy and we went through the same thing at the same time together, but that's about it. Like Law says, there's an event that divides everyone's timeline, and Brody was before my parents' death. He left a few months before the car accident, so he belongs to my old life. When my parents died, I became an adult a lot faster than planned, and I've always seen Brody as a big part of my childhood I left behind.

His laughter dies down enough for him to get out, "You had a random hook-up with a guy who ended up being an identical twin to a guy you kinda work with. You befriended the teacher, are still sleeping with his brother, but you woke up on your couch two days ago wrapped up in the straight guy. Did I get that right or am I confused? Because that's delightfully messy."

Messy doesn't begin to cover it, and I have no idea what I'm doing. With Anders or Law.

Something changed between Law and me the other night. Or maybe I'm reading into it. Fuck, why does he have to be the straight one? He's perfect. A little damaged, but aren't we all?

The thing that's worrying me the most is even after hearing Anders' story from Law, Law is the one I want to be there for. I want to pick up his broken pieces. Shouldn't the guy I'm sleeping with be the one I want to look out for?

Brody's easy smile is begging to be wiped off his face.

"You know," I say, "if you hadn't avoided me for the first few weeks of me being here, I wouldn't have had to play nice with others."

"Where's my entertainment in that? Besides, I … I didn't know how it was going to be … seeing you again after five years."

"You left me."

"You could've come with me."

"Are we really going to get into this?" I ask. "We agreed to be friends when you left for uni. High school relationships rarely work out as it is, let alone ones that have to endure long distance. And being closeted."

"Two and a half hours isn't long distance. It's … an annoyance. And you could've come here for uni too."

I shake my head. "God, if I'd done that, I never would've forgiven myself leaving Mum and Dad and losing them only a few months later."

Brody's smile turns grim. "I'm sorry I wasn't there for you when that happened."

God, I don't want to talk about my parents right now.

"We made the right choice back then, and it's not like you have feelings for me anymore." I swallow hard. "Right?"

"Honestly? I was worried it might all come back when I saw you, but the truth is, you're butt ugly now you've aged."

And just like that, it's easy between us again. "Thanks, man." I wish I could say the same about him, but that would be a lie. He fills out a suit nicely, and his brown messy hair contrasts the stuffy lawyer vibe his suit gives out. "I bet the only reason you get laid is because you work for the biggest criminal law firm in Australia. Guys see dollar signs."

He knows I'm lying and smirks. "Do you want my honest opinion?" Brody asks. Before I can answer, he keeps talking. Guess it was a rhetorical question then. "You need to end it with the hook-up. It's just sex, yeah?"

"Yeah. He's not very talkative."

"Lucky bastard," Brody says. "Where can I find a guy who doesn't talk and blows me?"

"Get your own. Anders is mine."

"But he's not the one you want."

"I could want him," I argue. "If we got to know each other outside of bed. Maybe."

"Answer me something. When you're with Anders, who are you picturing?"

"Anders." I think.

"When you're with the other one—"

"Law."

"Law … seriously who are their parents? Their names are just plain mean."

"Hey, at least they're not named after a weed." Reed is not a fun name to grow up with.

"True. Maybe they're your match. Maybe they're into twin—"

"If you say kinky twin shit, I'm leaving."

Brody smiles. "I'm wondering if you're projecting the relationship you want with Anders onto Law. Anders gives you the physical stuff, the other gives you all the horrible shit like common interests and"—he shudders—"intimacy."

I gasp. "You said a bad word. You haven't changed at all. Still emotionally stunted."

"Yes, but my big dick makes up for it."

"If you say so."

It's great to be laughing and joking around with Brody again like old times, but I don't want to admit he's hit the nail on the head. Anders and I have fun, but I'm connected to Law on a whole other level. We're passionate about the same things. Even though he was reliving his own personal hell the other night, he stayed by Davis's side when he didn't have to. He's a great teacher, selfless, and isn't too serious all the time. We have fun too, just not the same type of fun I have with his brother. Law is the type of guy I want to be with. I wonder if I'm letting Anders continually come over because he can give me what his brother can't. Or maybe it's the other way around and I'm taking from Law what I want with Anders.

"You look like you're going to throw up," Brody says.

"You look like someone who's about to be punched."

Brody laughs. "I'd like to see you try."

"Hey, I'm learning karate. I might be able to kick your ass."

He reaches across the table with his long arm and pats my head. "Sure you could."

I ball my napkin up and throw it at him. "Asshole."

"You've missed me," he quips.

"A little. It's good to have my best friend back."

He winces at the seriousness of my tone, and I revel in it.

"Aww, is this mushy shit killing your masculinity?"

"Fuck you."

Yep, it's definitely good to see Brody again.

The guy I'm ninety percent sure is Anders stands outside my apartment when I arrive home from dinner. He spins on his heel and gives me his assessing half-smile. It's as if he's waiting for me to decide which twin he'll be. There's a moment of hesitance each time he's turned up here. Like he's testing me. He doesn't want to be the one to tell me who he is. I hate to admit it, but the only reason I always thought it was him was because Law didn't know where I lived. Now he does.

"Sorry, I should've messaged," he says. "You been out?"

I clear my throat. "Just to dinner."

He frowns but recovers so fast I wonder if I imagine it. I *want* him to be jealous of my dinner, but I still don't know for sure who I'm staring at, so do I want Anders or Law to be jealous? I have no idea.

"Hot date?"

"If it was?"

He shrugs and looks at his feet. "Then I'm doing a shit job of keeping you happy. I mean, I know we're casual, but …"

At his insecurity, the tension in my chest snaps. I step forward and cup the back of his head, bringing his lips to mine.

Yeah, I was hoping it was Anders.

That's what I tell myself as I blindly unlock my door and enter my apartment still attached to Anders' face.

The usual tightening of my jeans doesn't happen right away, and I would blame the wine I had at dinner, except for the fact Anders' lips feel … weird. Wrong.

No, Brody's just got in my head. That's all.

Anders is perfect for me and what I need right now, which is still no strings attached. I'm not looking for a boyfriend. Nope. Not at all. Not interested in falling for someone, coming home to someone …

Fuck. I *do* want that. But do I want it with Anders?

He's hot, the sex is off the charts, and the most important thing—he's gay. Aside from that, I know shit all about him apart from what Law's told me, and it speaks volumes that Anders hasn't trusted me with his past or told me anything personal.

Anders pulls back. "Are you okay?"

Guess I'm not showing my usual level of eagerness to get him naked. "Yeah, I am. Umm, could we maybe sit for a bit? Talk?"

"O … kaaay."

I can do this. I can have "real talk" with Anders.

He throws himself on my couch. "What did you want to talk about?"

"How's Law?"

Anders cocks his brow. "You want to talk about Law when we could be having sex right now?"

"Umm, I guess not. How's work?"

"It's accounting. It's fucking boring."

I laugh. "Okay, won't talk about that either."

"Good. Talking portion of the night over yet?" He slides closer, putting his arm around my shoulder and moving his head closer to mine.

Anders has a point. Talking isn't what we're together for. We're not a sit on the couch type of couple, watching brainless movies and picking out giant plot holes. No, I have that with his straight brother.

Dammit, I want Law.

Brody's right. I need to end this.

There's no chance of ever being with Law, but being with Anders while thinking of his brother is the most asshole thing I could possibly do in this situation. Breaking up with Anders might make Law hate me, but if he knew the kinds of thoughts running through my head right now as Anders' hand slides down my chest on a rapid descent towards my cock, I'm pretty sure Law would hate me even more.

"I have a confession," I blurt out and pull away from Anders. I stand and pace the room, my heavy feet thudding along the hardwood floors, and I can feel Anders' eyes as they track my every move.

How am I supposed to tell him I can't be with him because he reminds me too much of his brother? And that I like Law more.

"What's wrong?" he asks.

"That dinner tonight. I lied. It was a date—"

"It's okay. We haven't promised each other anything." Anders' hand does this shaking, trembling thing, and I don't know if it's from anger or nerves. I wonder if he knows where this is going.

I run a hand over my hair and force myself to spit out lies. "This guy … I really like him. It's wrong being with you when I want to make it work with him."

Yeah, I've taken the chicken way out, but there's no point telling Anders I'm falling for his brother. With hope, when I stop messing around with Anders, my crush on Law will disappear because no weird lines will be crossed where I'm hooking up with his look-a-like.

Anders stands. "Right. Okay then." He shuffles from one foot to the other awkwardly. "Well … I, umm, guess it was fun while it lasted." Anders has this fidgeting tic—the same one Law has when his brother is mentioned.

"I'm sorry," I say. "Yell at me if you need to."

"Not necessary. I'm, ah, I'll go. See ya 'round."

Shit, I didn't expect to see genuine hurt in his eyes.

"I really am sorry," I call after him, but his feet don't stop. If anything, he walks faster.

Maybe I should go after him and explain the truth, but what good would that do? Plus, he might tell his brother about the whole crush thing, and while I've never had a serious thing for a straight guy before, I can't see how telling Law would be a good idea. Maybe I should go after Anders and tell him I changed my mind, but that's a slippery slope. Ending it now is what's best for everyone involved, even if some parties are unknowingly the thing coming between me and Anders.

I stay frozen to the spot, unable to determine just how much I'm going to regret my decision tomorrow.

12

LAWSON

Anders takes a swing, but I duck and pivot.

"Spill it, brother." He breathes heavy, preparing to try to attack me again.

I grunt. "Maybe you should focus on your advances instead of what's going on with me."

"You've been a cranky asshole for days, and now you're trying to beat the shit out of me. Your fuck buddy situation go south already? She find out your name's Lawson, not Dawson?"

"What do you care? Watch my attacks, dammit." I almost sock him in the face because he's not paying attention.

"Why won't you tell me about her?"

"Why don't you shut the hell up before I shut you up."

Anders laughs because he knows I'm bluffing. I don't hit my brother, even when sparring. At least, not on purpose.

The smartass takes me off-guard and tackles me, turning my serious training into a wrestling match.

"You're a bastard," I say and roll on top of him.

"Did someone bweak my poor wittle bwother's heart?" he mocks, while trying to fight me off.

Yes. "Fuck off."

Anders pulls strength from who knows where and pushes me away. He pins me to the mats and straddles me. He captures my wrists in his palms and pins them to the mats too. "Seriously, bro. What's wrong?"

The fight leaves me as I try to sink into the floor. "I got dumped." And it stings way more than it should. Reed and I weren't even together—not officially. It was just sex. He thought I was Anders, for Christ's sake. What we had wasn't real.

Then why does it hurt so fucking much? When he told me he had a thing for the guy he had dinner with—whoever he is—I should've been elated. It gave us the simple out I needed. Everything wouldn't turn to shit, and I'd still get to be friends with him as myself.

But I never planned on falling for the guy, which evidently, I did.

Now what am I supposed to do?

Anders laughs and collapses beside me.

"So hilarious," I say.

"Just talk to her. The wrong name isn't a big deal."

"Nah, it's not that. We were casual and … there was someone else." Avoiding pronouns is hard.

I'll tell Anders eventually about the fact I like guys. When, I don't know, but it doesn't feel like something I should just blurt out like he did. Especially because I've kept it hidden for so long.

When Anders had come out to me, it was as simple as

him saying some guy at school was hot. For a second, I thought he knew about me and was fishing. To cover my ass, I answered vaguely with, "If you're into that sort of thing." He replied, "Yeah … I, uh, am."

In retrospect, this was the moment I was supposed to say *me too*. Instead, my heart was too busy frantically beating its way out of my chest because the thought of both of us being queer seemed wrong. Whether it was the stigma of what that meant back then or if it was the twin thing, I'm not sure. I imagined disappointing our parents and people saying ridiculous things like they raised us that way. I made a choice back then to stay quiet, because I wasn't lying or pretending to be something I wasn't when I was with women. And it worked. It's only been recently that I've wanted to explore my interest in guys.

Now that I know what I've been missing, there's no way I'm going back to only dating girls.

Ungh. The thought of dating at all makes my gut churn. I don't want to date anyone else—male or female. I want Reed.

Anders nudges me. "Then she's not worth it."

"Let's call it. You have to get back to work, and I have afternoon classes coming in soon." One of them being Reed's class.

Anders doesn't usually train on a Monday, so I haven't had to worry about him running into Reed, but he skipped last week and wanted to make up for it today. I need to make sure he's out of here before my students turn up.

What's worse than the thought of them running into each other is the fact I'm going to have to pretend like Reed didn't dump my ass for someone else, because he didn't. He broke up with Anders. Technically.

How did I ever think this was going to work? Granted, I didn't realise I'd started to like Reed more than a hook-up and friend until he told me we couldn't have sex anymore, but what was my real long-term plan? Fuck him out of my system and then just look at Reed as a co-worker? I can't ghost someone I have to see every single week.

Anders grabs a quick shower in my private bathroom off the side of my office and then goes back to work while I set up for the afternoon classes.

I have to mentally psych myself up to face Reed and pretend I'm cool with him.

When he walks through the door with the kids in tow, I can't bring myself to look at him.

"Head on through. I'll be there in a minute," I say to no one and pretend to be busy behind the counter. My appointments and schedule need straightening out. That'd sound legit if he asked.

I sense a presence looming over me, but I don't raise my head. That is until Davis says, "Law?"

My gaze flies up to meet his. The bruise on his face is already healed, but that was the least of his injuries. I'm interested to know what his torso looks like. "How … how is everything?"

He averts his eyes. "Good. Thanks to you. Mr. Garvey said I should thank you again—"

"I don't need thanks. Just knowing you're safe is thanks enough for me."

"I am. Mum left Dad. Like officially and stuff. Signed separation papers or whatever they're called."

"I know it's probably not what you want to hear, but … it might be for the best. You need to surround yourself with people who'll support you and build you up, not criticise you for who you are or who you like."

Davis nods but doesn't seem convinced. "He's still my dad, you know? I guess part of me is hoping he'll wake up and realise he lost both me and Mum because of what he did, and he'll apologise and want to make amends. I want him to …"—he breathes deep—"I still want him to accept me. That's fucked up, isn't it?"

"Language," Reed says from the bamboo doorway to the classroom.

Davis looks at his feet. "Sorry. Just, thank you again."

"No problem at all." My heart breaks for the kid. Mum and Dad didn't give a shit when Anders came out, and I assume they'll be the same when I do. Imagining not having their support …

I try to stop Davis to say something reassuring—what, I have no idea—but it's too late. He heads inside, and Reed still stands in the doorway, staring at me. Our eyes lock. His golden hair shines off the overhead lights, and in his gi, he looks like an ass-kicking angel dude. I wish he wasn't hot.

"Anders told you, didn't he?" he says, his tone defeated.

"Uh, yeah. But hey, it's none of my business." I go back to looking at the open ledger in front of me, pretending to focus on words when all I can focus on is my tongue thick in my mouth and my dry throat.

"Are we cool? Like, not just about Anders, but about the whole … waking up together on my couch thing."

"We're cool." I shrug, trying to be nonchalant but my shoulders are stiff.

"We still on for our usual dinner tonight?"

Shit. I don't think I could stand it. "Sorry. Not tonight. I promised Anders I'd be home."

"Right. Got it. You told me that first night we met that you were protective of your brother, but trust me when I say I didn't mean to hurt him or lead him on. I have my reasons for ending it, and I hope it doesn't come between me and you." He turns on his heel and heads back into the classroom.

Part of me wants to explain why I'm distant, but it wouldn't do any good. He's dating that other guy. Plus, I never had any faith that he'd forgive what I did. No, the fantasy in my head where I explain everything and he tells me he doesn't care will never come true, and I have to accept that.

He's only ever seen me as a friend, and why would he see me as anything else? When I was half out of it and kissed him that one time as me, he was mortified. Which is a normal reaction to your pseudo-boyfriend's brother kissing you, I guess. But it stung.

During class, I don't include Reed like I normally do. There's a pinch in my gut and longing in my chest. My mood is sombre, and I think the kids pick up on it too. And when I dismiss the class early, it gets a round of moans and complaints.

I rub my temples because this sucks.

"Come on, guys," Reed says. "Law has a headache."

Yeah, I do—his name is Reed, and I think I'm in love with him.

Fuck. Love? Really?

I've known the guy a total of what, a few weeks? A

month? That's nowhere near long enough to use the L word. It doesn't matter that he touches me in a way no woman ever has. His drive, his passion for teaching, and the sex—oh God, the sex—these are all reasons I like him. But the way he stayed calm during the Davis situation, the way he held my hand, offered me a place to sleep, and then stayed up half the night with me watching shitty movies so I didn't have to think or go back into a nightmare—that's why I love him.

I think I knew it the morning I woke up next to him on his couch, but I wasn't ready to admit it to myself, so I ran out of there without much of an explanation.

It's also why I can't stand to be around him anymore and why being friends with him won't work.

I didn't realise I was falling for him until it was too late. This was supposed to end with Reed yelling at me for being a lying douche, not me wanting to crumple to a heap on the floor.

I need to either tell him the truth and make him hate me or find a way to act normal around him instead of all emo-like. But I don't want Reed to hate me.

The kids file out of the room, and I hope and pray Reed follows soon after, but he doesn't.

I hold my breath, waiting for him to say something, but we stare at each other, unblinking, and I have no idea where to go from here.

"Can we go to dinner another night this week?" he asks. The strain in his voice kills me, and it takes everything in me not to say I'd give him anything and everything he wants if he just takes me back.

"I'll see what I can do."

He knows I'm lying. With a huff, he leaves the dojo, and I sink to my ass on the floor.

To him, he only lost a fuck buddy. He thinks I'm pissed because of my protectiveness over Anders. He has no idea that I'm completely fucking heartbroken, because for the first time in my life, I was with someone I could see a future with.

But that future isn't possible, because I keep forgetting one very important part. He doesn't know who I truly am.

This whole situation is fucked up.

All week, I try to get Reed out of my head. I try to prepare for acting like a normal human when I see him. It's useless. I have no idea when or how it happened for me to be this far gone for a guy, but it's affecting every part of my life.

My eyes sting from lack of sleep, and I'm living on coffee and bourbon. It's a vicious cycle. I have coffee because I wake up exhausted from restless nights, drink two shots of whisky to make me pass out for a while, and then wake up in a sweat a few hours later. The alcohol is probably making it worse, but it's the only thing that helps me drift off at all.

Because I've ignored Reed's messages throughout the week, when he arrives the following Monday for class, he doesn't acknowledge me. I'm both thankful and pissed off for it.

I manage to pull the class together and act relatively upbeat for the kids, but Davis's eyes keep ping-ponging between Reed and me. We might be fooling ourselves, but we're not fooling him.

My suspicions are confirmed when Davis approaches me after class.

"Why are you and Mr. Garvey fighting?"

"We're not," I say.

"Liar. Has it … it got anything to do with how you helped me—"

"Nothing to do with you. I promise."

Reed's voice comes from the doorway. "I was dating his brother, and we broke up. Law's pissed at me."

"You have to stop eavesdropping," I say.

"Rules. Not allowed to leave you alone with a student. I'm just doing my job."

"Well, you two need to sort your shit out," Davis says.

"Language," Reed scolds. I don't know why he keeps trying to tone down Davis's swearing, but it's cute when he does. I hate that.

"Just sayin'. You guys are sucking the fun out of class. So kiss and make up."

I wince.

"We'll sort it," Reed says. "But right now, you need to get on the bus." Reed meets my eyes. "I'll message you later."

I manage a small nod and then let out my breath when they finally leave.

When will this get easier?

Across the room, my phone lights up with a text

message, but my next class starts filing in, so I don't get a chance to read it.

I get back in my groove—the under-fives tend to make me smile because they're adorable when they shout a kiai—but by the time my last class rolls around, I'm ready for home.

What I don't expect is Anders to walk through my door to join in. It's an adult class, so that's fine, but he's not a joiner. We usually do one-on-one training.

"Didn't you get my message?" he asks at my puzzled expression.

"I haven't had a chance to check my phone. What are you doing here?"

He shrugs and looks away.

"Anders ..." I warn.

"I'm making sure you're okay, because you're clearly not. I know the signs of someone struggling. I've lived them, and you were there for me each and every time I fell apart. I don't know why this chick is different to the other women you date or why you're so cut up over it ending, but I'm gonna make sure I'm here if you need me. So now I'm your student."

Bloody hell. "I haven't been that bad."

"You're not sleeping, bro."

True, but that's because my nightmares have come back. Most nights I relive finding Anders, but the past two nights, it's been Reed I see all bloodied. I haven't been able to talk to anyone about it because that would involve bringing Anders down with me, and he's been doing so well.

If it's bad enough that Anders is noticing, and Davis, for that matter, I guess it's time I did something about it.

"I'll tell you everything after class," I say, and I mean it. I'll tell him everything. I'm not afraid to come out to him. My closeted status has never been about that. I mean, there's the nervous feeling of wanting to throw up, but I think that just comes with the territory of telling your brother you've kept something hidden from him for over a decade. I know he won't care that I like guys and girls. Thanks to Reed, I can say that with absolutely no hesitation or confusion.

I am worried how Anders will react when he finds out I pretended to be him for a month so I could keep sleeping with my co-worker, though. Putting it that way makes me sound like a psycho. This is going to be a long conversation, so there's no way I can blurt it out now when I'm about to lead a half-hour class.

"Whenever you're ready." Anders condescendingly pats my cheek.

My foot kicks out to the side and swings around the back of his legs, swiping them out from underneath him.

He lands on his back with a thud. "Guess I deserved that."

Those already in the room laugh, and others enter the room and do a double take when they see Anders and me. Twin shit—people are always fascinated by it for some reason. I don't get it.

I don't want to admit it, but having Anders front row for my class calms me somewhat and distracts me from everything going on in my messed-up head. It's also reassuring to know that my brother has my back, just as I have his. It didn't occur to me how much of a one-way street my relationship with Anders has been until Reed asked me who's there for me when I need someone. I've been fine to be the one who's had to keep it together because what Anders went through is so much worse than what I endured, but neither of us realised his attack had a ripple effect. He wasn't the only one who almost died that night.

If I'd lost my brother, my literal other half, I wouldn't have survived it. Mum and Dad worry about us, even now, years later. Dad hides it better than Mum, but whenever we go home, it's always a tense environment when Kyle is mentioned or something from years ago comes back to haunt us.

As we cool down from the class, doing last-minute stretches, I take a deep breath and prepare myself to lay it all out there for Anders. He might be shocked at first—especially when he finds out I've known I liked guys basically my whole life—but I know he'll support me. Telling him about Reed on the other hand … he'll either laugh his ass off or be pissed at me. It's an unwritten law between twins. Don't pretend to be the other without permission.

Anders starts packing away the mats while I see everyone out. "The faster we get this done, the sooner we can hit a bar."

"It's a Monday."

He shrugs. "I have a feeling this talk is going to need alcohol."

Well, he has a point there.

I join him in cleaning up when everyone leaves, and about five minutes later, I'm vaguely aware of the storefront door opening, but I'm too much of a dumbass to think it's anyone but a returning customer who's forgotten something.

"Law?"

I stiffen at Reed's voice but am thinking clearly enough to do a quick analysis of the situation. I'm wearing my gi, but the real Anders is wearing a singlet shirt where you can see he doesn't have my shoulder tattoo, and he's also wearing his eyebrow ring that, in reality, he rarely takes out.

When Reed steps through the bamboo curtain, his eyes find me first and then Anders. Unlike my students who double take from being in the same room as two guys who look identical, Reed steps back for a whole other reason. He watches an invisible tennis match between me and Anders.

Time slows down and it's drawn out further by no one saying anything.

This is all about to come out, and not in the way I was hoping. I have no control over this situation.

Reed finally asks, "Are you guys triplets or something?"

At the same time, Anders matches Reed's confusion. "Who are you?"

Ah, fuck. I stand completely still, unable to speak or run away. Running away sounds perfect right now, if only I could get my feet to move.

"Triplets?" Anders asks.

"Well, yeah, you're not Anders or Law."

"Reed," I say but can't find more words.

"Law, what is he talking—wait, I know you," Anders says. "You were my date. My date that—"

"I can explain." I don't want to, but I don't have any other option right now. Running out of here won't work unless I plan on never coming back. I've heard New Zealand is nice this time of year.

Reed's eyebrows go from being drawn together to

soaring sky high the exact moment he works it out. Though impossible, I swear I see his heart shatter. "Law, please tell me I'm jumping to all the wrong conclusions here when I assume you're the guy I've been fucking."

"What?" Anders blanches. "He's straight."

I don't know who to address first. "No, bro. I'm really not. I need to explain—"

Reed crosses the room and pulls open my gi, exposing my tattoo. Stumbling back, he looks at Anders' eyebrow. "You two are sick."

"Whoa, dude," Anders says. "You don't even know me."

"Anders," I say. "Not now. I need to—"

Reed shakes his head. "I can't believe … I … fuck this. I'm out. Don't come near me. Either of you." He storms out, and I watch him go. Each footstep closer to the exit he gets, my heart cracks open a little more.

Anders calls after him. "What did I do?"

This is the last thing I wanted. I didn't want to hurt Reed, but I knew all along it was inevitable if I kept seeing him. Yet, I did it anyway, because I can't stay away from him. I don't want to.

My feet hesitate for only a few seconds. "Reed." I run after him. He's almost at his car when I catch up. "Wait. I need to—"

He spins on his heel. "That's why you disappeared when I broke it off with Anders? Because I unknowingly broke up with *you*?"

My mouth drops open, but again, I can't find the right words. Everything I say is going to hurt him in one way or another.

"I didn't mean for it to get that far," I whisper. "I tried to tell you."

Reed folds his arms across his chest. "Why didn't you?"

"Well … usually because your tongue ended up in my mouth."

His lips quirk but he recovers quickly. "This is fucked up, Law."

"I know."

My gaze doesn't drop from his, even though his eyes bore right into me, trying to figure out if there's any good inside.

"I'm not that guy—the one who does shit like this."

A group of people walk by us on the narrow sidewalk, pushing me closer to Reed. If I wasn't ruined enough, he destroys me by stepping backwards—as if he could sink into his car—like he can't get away from me fast enough.

"It was only supposed to be that first night," I say. "Then I found out I work with you, and I didn't know how to tell you. I figured if you knew the truth you'd want nothing to do with me, and I couldn't handle that. But you ran anyway when you met that other guy."

"What other guy?"

"Your date guy."

Guilt flashes across his face, and he averts his gaze.

"Yeah," I say, feeling used. It may be a double standard because I was using Reed too. Difference is, for me it only started out that way. I've fallen for him. I've fallen hard. "Obviously you didn't feel anything for me. Or Anders." Low blow, maybe, but fuck, I'm grasping at straws. I need a reason to be mad at him—like it could even the playing field and lessen my fuckup somehow.

"You *are* Anders! You pretended to be your brother to have sex with me and then pretended to be my friend in between. You need professional help. That's like psycho level of … psychoness."

I want to so badly call him out for being an English teacher who just used the word *psychoness*, but I know now's not the time. That's a joke between friends, and we are not friends right now. "I'm sorry" is all I manage to say. "I didn't know how to stop."

"It's too late for sorry."

When he walks around his car and opens the driver's side door, I beg for him to stop. Whether it's aloud or silent, I don't know, because he either doesn't hear me or ignores me no matter how loud I plead.

I watch the empty street long after he's turned the corner and gone from my life. When I head back inside the dojo, Anders is where I left him, still packing away the mats and equipment.

He looks up when he senses me, and stands taller, awaiting my explanation, but words fail me.

I can't catch my breath.

I've really lost him. Reed's gone.

I fall to my knees and bend forward. My elbows hit the mats as I hang my head.

"Law?" My brother sinks down beside me. "Is there something you're not telling me? Something about accidentally wandering into my closet and rummaging around?"

"Fuck," I mutter into the mats. Trust Anders to make a joke right now. "I know I should've told you, but it's new. I mean … no, it's not new." Sitting up, I give my brother the respect he deserves by staring him in the eyes as I say this.

"I've always known I'm bi, but I just never … I never dated guys because—"

"Because that's my thing."

I nod, no longer able to keep looking at him.

Anders sighs and it's full of resignation and understanding. "I'm not going to say you're an idiot, even if you are. We try to stand apart from each other in so many ways, but it's a stupid thing to keep hidden from me. Did you think I'd react badly to this?"

"It's not that. Yeah, it might be a little messed up that I didn't want to date guys because of you, but it's not why I didn't do it. I was fine with not having to label it or focus on it or make it a big deal. I've been confident in my skin for a long time but have only just started to explore that side of me. And Reed …"

Anders screws up his face. "He thinks you're me? No wonder that dude is pissed."

"It started the night I was supposed to break off your date with him. It was a hook-up and I was never going to see him again."

"Have you ever done that before? Like gone home with one of my—"

"Fuck no. Uh … no offence."

Anders chuckles.

"It turns out we work together—me and Reed. In this dojo, I'm Law, so I couldn't pretend to be you when he knew you were an accountant. Before I knew it, I was friends with him as Law but fucking him as Anders. I'd go to his place and he always assumed I was you when he answered the door. I'm a coward for not telling him, but I knew I'd lose him in the end." I rub my chest. "I just didn't think it'd hurt this much."

"Whoa, you really like this guy."

Yeah, I do, and I fucked it up. "Doesn't matter anyway, because he dumped you for another guy."

"You're gonna ruin my rep, bro. Anders doesn't get broken up with. You should remember that for next time."

"Next time? Don't think it'll happen again. Reed's the only date of yours I've actually liked."

Anders laughs.

"You're … You're not mad?"

"I can see why you'd want to be me, because well, I'm better than you. And while I hope you don't have to use my name to get your rocks off—because that would need serious therapy—it's not like you hurt anyone. It's not a big deal, Law."

"Thanks for the perspective, but I did hurt someone. I hurt Reed every time I pretended to be you."

"Hey, at least you didn't try to slit his throat."

I wince. I should be grateful he can say such things without freaking out now, but it still reminds me of how I found him. I stare at my bloodied hands and try to wash away the invisible red like I've done a thousand times before.

Anders slaps my hands away from each other. "All I mean is Reed might not forgive you for being a douche, and I'm not saying what you did was right, but honestly? Don't feel guilty about it. It was a mistake that snowballed into more. Doing one bad thing doesn't make you a bad person."

"Then why does it feel so shitty?"

"I'm actually kinda glad it happened. Makes you more

human when you screw up. That's usually my job. Do you know how hard it is living in your shadow?"

Finally, I manage a smile. "Wait ... can you repeat that? I think I need to record it."

Anders' tone shifts and gets weighted with his I'm-not-fucking-around attitude. "Not only are you doing something to contribute to society here"—he waves his hand around the dojo—"you were there for me through everything. You break up with guys for me with only minor complaint because you can't stand to see me struggle, and I can't help thinking you wouldn't have been in this position if it weren't for me. Maybe you would've met Reed on your own at work and fell for him as yourself."

"But then I might not have had the guts to go for it. Guess it's better it all came out sooner rather than later. At least now I don't have to pretend to be mad at him for breaking up with you. I'm angry because he left *me*."

"You're in love with him," my brother says.

"Am not." The words feel thick as they fall from my mouth, because I know I'm lying. The truth is, I don't want to love Reed because there's no chance in hell he'd ever forgive me after what I did.

"You can't lie to me."

I raise my eyebrow. "Oh, I can't? How's this for not being able to lie to you—this thing with Reed has been going on for a month."

"Okay, so you were able to keep him a dirty little secret, but I knew something was up with you. I just thought it was chick problems, and we all know how unhelpful I am with that type of plumbing."

I snort.

"How are you going to get him back?" Anders asks.

"Not gonna happen. Even if he was willing to forgive me, he's with someone else. Not to mention his ex is a lying asshole, and I've done exactly the same thing. The best I can hope for is for him not to hate me and we can be friends ... I guess." The thought of having to go to dinner with Reed and his new boyfriend makes me cringe. Maybe the best we can hope for is being civil during work hours. One hour a week; that might be doable.

"Can I ask something that will probably piss you off?" my brother asks.

"You're you. You'll do that anyway."

"Truth." Anders sighs and looks away. "If Reed were a woman, would you give in so easily?"

"Fuck you."

"Told you, you wouldn't like it. But my point is, you've put in more effort with women in the past—arguably when they didn't deserve it"—he coughs in between saying *Olivia*—"but here you are giving up on Reed easily even though it's obvious you're a wreck without him, and the only difference between your exes and him is he has a dick."

"He's dating someone else now," I argue. "What am I supposed to do? Break them up?"

"When you were with him as me, did you act like you or me? Because if you tried to act like me as well as use my name, then I can kinda understand why he'd choose the other guy, but now he knows it was you pretending to be me ..."

I grunt and get to my feet. "I'm done talking about this. It's over. Done."

Anders hesitates before nodding once. "If that's how you

want to play it, but this conversation is not done. Still want to go to a bar tonight?"

"Nah, I just wanna go home."

"Probably for the best. We've never had to deal with cutting each other's grass before. Might cause fights."

"Except I'm really not into twinks. Broke up with too many of them for you."

"Should be no problems then." He grins.

13

REED

Brody's laugh echoes as if he has me on speakerphone. He better not. I don't want anyone overhearing how stupid I am. "The guy you broke up with because you were falling for his brother is actually the brother?"

"Why do you find my life hilarious?"

"You chose the wrong subject to teach. You should be teaching drama."

"When you're done, can you tell me what I do now?"

Brody's laughter dies. "I thought that'd be obvious. Be with the guy you've wanted—and had—all along."

"He lied to me about who he was for a month." I pace my small living room and run a hand through my hair.

"Hmm, yeah, douche move. Why did he do it?"

"Who knows."

"You didn't ask? Maybe he had a good reason. Like … umm … okay, I can't think of any reason why he'd do that."

"I think I was a sexual experiment. He's straight."

"Clearly not. And why couldn't he do that as himself? Why pretend to be his brother?"

"I don't know."

"Maybe they did a whole parent trap style switcheroo to mess with you?"

"I'm under the impression real Anders had no idea Law and I were seeing each other, so it's not like they did this for fun. Not together at least. But Law doesn't seem like the type to fuck with people for entertainment."

There's a knock at the door, and I freeze in my steps. My heart rate kicks up a notch as if it knows who's behind that knock. Part of me hopes Deb has an emergency and it's not who I think it is. I can't face him. I will never be able to face him.

"Reed, let me in."

Dammit. "Brody, I gotta go."

"Is that him?"

"Yup." I hit end on the call, and when I open my front door, I narrow my eyes. "What are *you* doing here?"

"We need to talk." He pushes past me.

"Rude much?"

"I need to explain about what happened. It has a lot to do with my brother and what he's been through."

I fold my arms across my chest. "Oh?"

"Anders has issues."

I laugh and mumble, "That's understating it." I examine the man's features closely as he chews on his bottom lip—something Law has never done before. His stance is all wrong, he's more nervous and twitchy than the Law I know, and there's something about him that I can't put my finger on. All I know is, this isn't my Law standing in front of me.

"You have to understand. Anders … he—"

"Cut the bullshit, *Anders*," I say. "I know it's you."

"How?" A finger rubs over where his piercing should be.

"I know Law inside and out. You look nothing like him."

"We're identical twins. Our own mother gets confused sometimes."

"What are you doing here?" What is it about the Steele brothers that makes me antsy, uncomfortable, and horny all at the same time? Wait, that's not entirely true. Standing here, eyeing the real Anders, there's no attraction to him whatsoever. He's not Law. The confusion between the two had always been present because it was Law the whole time. "How did you know where I live?"

"I got my client's address and knocked on two other doors before someone told me which one was yours. How much did Law tell you about me? When he was with you, I mean … as me."

I shrug. "Not a lot. My relationship with 'Anders' wasn't much more than physical. It was my relationship with Law that meant something …" Who's the same guy. No matter how many times the scenario plays out in my head, I can't get over the shock.

"Wait, so you do have a thing for Law? While you were with me, you were falling in love with my straight brother?"

"You and I were never together. And he's obviously not straight. What I don't understand is why he did it, why you're here, or why I'm even bothering listening to you. Do you do this type of shit often?"

He doesn't hesitate in answering. "Yes."

"Get out."

"No. Not until you let me explain. That date with you

wasn't the first time Law has had to pretend to be me. Did he tell you what happened a few years ago?"

I shift from one foot to the other. "A little. That an ex tried to kill you."

"I still have issues because of it. The night I was supposed to meet you, I called Law in full on meltdown mode. I couldn't breathe, I swore I was having a heart attack, and I couldn't ... I couldn't face you, because you weren't what I was expecting. You're stocky, and—"

"Too old for you. I know. That's one thing Law did tell me. I'm not your type."

"You would've been if it wasn't for Kyle. Your physique reminded me of him, and it only took one glance at you to induce a panic attack. I can't allow myself to go for the guys I truly want, because ..." Anders blows out a loud breath. "Kyle fucked me up big time."

I want to hate Anders, but I can't help feeling sorry for the guy. "I'm sorry that you went through that, but I still don't see what any of this has to do with Law meeting me that night."

"I didn't have your phone number, I couldn't call or text to cancel, and standing you up would've been a dick move. I'm not that much of an asshole. I asked my brother to break off the date for me, and whenever I have an ... *episode*, if you will, Law is there to get me through it. I'm ashamed to admit he's broken up with a lot of guys for me because I can't handle conflict. He was supposed to walk in, tell you something came up, and then leave again, but—from what little detail he's given me—he wanted more. He'd never been with another guy before you."

While I suspected as much ever since I found out the

truth, it kills me that I didn't know sooner—that he didn't trust me. He hasn't only been keeping his identity from me, but personal shit I should know; especially if we're hooking up. "That doesn't make what he did acceptable, and it also pisses me off. I should get to decide if I want to be someone's sexual experiment."

"I agree—although, you got sex out of it, so I don't know why you're complaining—but he didn't know he was going to have to work with you. That first night was a hookup. You even said it yourself."

"How do you know?"

"After we left the dojo, I kept bugging him for an explanation. We just had a long talk, and he told me everything. At least, I think it's everything."

"Then why are you here and not him? And why did you pretend to be him when you first walked in the door?"

"Do you think I like the fact that because of me you and Law didn't get a proper chance? Had he met you through work like he was supposed to, none of this would've happened. I came over to make it right, and pretending to be Law … it's just easier if I'm not me when talking about real shit. I think the fact I didn't immediately run away when you called me out is what my therapist would call a breakthrough."

My eyes widen. "What would you have done if I forgave 'Law' and tried to kiss you? Do you and your brother think *anything* through?"

Anders shrugs. "I probably would've feigned stomach issues and ran away. I came here to make you see why you should dump that other loser—wait, is there another guy or did you break up with me because you were falling for Law?"

"Why should I give him another chance to fuck me over?" I ignore his question, because he's right.

Anders winces. "I don't need to know what you and my brother did in the bedroom."

I sigh. They're so much alike but so different.

"You should give him another chance, because he didn't purposefully set out to hurt you. He didn't mean to fall for you either, but he did. He's been through so much with me—you won't believe some of the shit he's had to deal with—and I want to see him happy. He's never been happier than he has this last month, apart from having to deceive you. He asked for my advice a few weeks back, and I didn't have all the facts, so I gave him misinformed guidance, which, for some reason, he decided to take for once. I told him to keep going until the whole thing blows up in his face and then move on because I didn't think it was possible for his heart to be broken."

"Wow. That's really shitty advice."

"It's why I'm an accountant. Give me numbers over emotional shit any day. When Law cares about someone, you don't know the lengths this guy would go for that person. But he thinks you dumped him for another guy—"

"I didn't. You were right. I broke up with you, because I thought it was unfair to think of Law while I was with you. Uh, him." I rub my temples. "This is way too confusing."

"There's only one thing you need to know about Law. When he loves, he loves hard. The beard that Law hates?" Anders turns his head to the side. "He maintains his so he can break up with guys for me. It covers my scar." His finger trails down his jawbone.

I can barely see it, but there's a definite white line running through Anders' beard. You wouldn't see it if you weren't specifically looking for it. "I don't understand."

"My ex slit my throat ... well, tried to, but Law saved me."

"How? He said he found you when you were almost dead."

"The reason my scar only goes to here"—he points to the side of his jaw—"is because while I was being attacked, I lied. I said I was Law, and Kyle freaked out. He couldn't tell the difference between us."

"Even with the eyebrow piercing?"

"I only got it pierced two years ago when I started going out again." Anders shrugs. "Quarter-life crisis. But telling Kyle I was my brother scared him enough for him to snap out of his rage. Without Law, I know for a fact I'd be dead. After the attack, it was a few years before I even wanted to leave my apartment. The only time I did was to knock on Law's door. I had to move in with him and let him take care of me. I was a wreck for a long time. He doesn't want to break up with guys for me, but he also doesn't want to see me slip back into hermit mode where I don't talk to anyone at all. It's taken a long time, but I'm back to the guy I was before the attack ... with a few quirks that tend to pop up every now and then, like when I'm set up on a blind date."

"Panic attacks are quirks?"

"Out of everything I just said, *that* is what you got from it?"

"I know Law's a great guy. You don't need to sell me on

it. But I don't know if I can forgive him. I hate liars—I was with one for almost four years. I don't need another lying asshole in my life when I spent the last six months getting over the last one."

"If you've spent a month with my brother and don't know he's not a lying asshole, then maybe I was wrong in coming here to try to make things right. He's one of the worst liars in the world. You probably didn't notice because you weren't looking for it."

All those times Law would clam up or he or 'Anders' would twitch and stand awkwardly. Their *shared* tic.

I huff. I thought he was uncomfortable because of Anders' attack, but now I know it's because he was trying to cover up a lie.

"Law made a mistake and didn't know how to get out of it. Part of him didn't want to because he didn't want to lose you," Anders says. "If that doesn't prove to you he loves you … then … I guess I'll see myself out."

Anders gets to the door before I find my voice. "Just … I need time. To process shit."

With a nod, he walks out of my apartment, and I stare at the door wondering if I could really forgive a guy who pretended to be someone else so he could be with me.

The words play over and over in my head until they have no more meaning, and I'm left more confused than before.

My name is Reed, and I'm a cowardly coward. At least, that's what I'd say if they had a support group like AA for people who are too chickenshit to face an ex. If that's even what I can call Law. I have no idea what we are, were, or what he ever thought we were going to be. Did he think we could live forever with me thinking he was Anders?

I call in sick the Monday after everything goes down so I don't have to take the union kids to see Law. I ignore his *I'm sorry* and *please let me explain* texts and the two calls, mainly because he's still saved in my phone as Anders, and each time his name flashes on the screen, I get angry again.

Logic would say to change the name in my phone, but I don't; I want to stay mad at him, and my resolve is cracking. I'm holding on to any remaining anger that I can.

That bastard.

Deep down, I know what he did to me is a lot different than what my ex did to me, but it feels the same. It leaves me unsure of myself and in a weird state of wondering what I did wrong. But in this case, I know I did nothing wrong. I was oblivious to the whole damn thing.

Still, knowing all those times I was with Anders I was actually with Law ... it makes the memories of us shine brighter in my head somehow. A stupid warmth rushes through me at the thought of me and him, and I hate him a little more because of it.

When the following Monday rolls around, and there's been a full week of radio silence from the Steele brothers, I brace myself to be the bigger person and act civil during martial arts class. The thought of dropping the union occurred to me briefly, but the kids are more important than the issues I have with Law.

I can do this.

As soon as I walk through the doors of the dojo, my eyes find Law's and my feet stall in the middle of the walkway.

I can't do this.

One of the kids nudges me from behind, and that gets my feet walking. Instead of heading for the training room, though, my feet go in the direction of Law, as if I'm wearing steel-capped boots and he's a giant magnet.

His cheeks are hollow, and his eyes seem empty—lifeless. I wonder if he's slept about as well as I have these past two weeks.

"Hey." He casts his gaze down as he talks, and I hate that I'm the one doing that to him.

How fucked up is that? He screws me over, yet I'm the one feeling guilty.

Unresolved attraction puts me in my place. I was worried this would happen—that I'd get in Law's presence and my need for him would outweigh my anger. It wasn't his fault he lied to me in the beginning, and it's not as if I would've kept seeing him if he'd told me the truth. He should've told me that first night before anything happened, but once he didn't, there was no turning back. That doesn't negate the fact he kept sleeping with me.

How am I supposed to get past that?

"If you're going to yell at me, just do it already," Law says. "Otherwise, I have a class to teach."

My mouth drops open, but nothing comes out.

Law scoffs and storms past me, as if he has a right to be

pissed about me ignoring him. Maybe he does. I just need time for the crippling feeling of betrayal to go away.

"I'm trying," I say, and he pauses in his steps. "I want to get over it, but I don't at the same time. There was never anyone else. It was you. I broke up with your brother for *you*, even though I thought you were straight. I couldn't be with him when I was wishing he was someone else."

Law spins on his heel and tries to step closer to me, but I hold my hand up to stop him.

"But you broke us. You lied to me about who you were."

"I know," he whispers and hangs his head. "If I could do it all again, I would've told you in the restaurant that my brother sent me instead. You just … you seemed … *perfect*—everything I'd fantasised about and never allowed myself to have. I wanted that for a little while."

The least selfish person I know did a selfish thing for once because he never gets to be that guy. He has too much on his plate with Anders and the kids he teaches. "It just sucks that the one time you take something for yourself, you took something from me to have it."

Shit, with Law's eyes cast down, he doesn't only look guilty but completely heartbroken.

"And now you're looking at me like that and not playing fair."

He lifts his head and a tiny smile appears, but it doesn't last. "The second time we were together, I turned up on your doorstep to tell you, but then you kissed me, and all rationale flew out of my head. Every time I tried to tell you, something stopped me."

My solidifying heart defrosts a little at that, but it's still not enough. I don't know what it will take for me to get over it. Or if I can. I don't know whether it's because I can't trust him not to lie again or my ego is too wounded. All I know is I can't do it right now. "I just need time, and even then, I can't guarantee anything." I blow out a loud breath. "You hurt me. Not as Anders. As you. My friend and work colleague."

"I get that, and if it takes a thousand apologies, I'll do it. A million, even."

Davis calls out from the classroom. "Are we judoing or not?"

"Judoing isn't a word," Law and I yell at the same time. The shared laugh almost brings us back to normal.

"We should get in there," Law says, his tone defeated.

"Yeah …"

Before we can take any steps, the shopfront door swings open, and a staggering Mr. Sullivan appears. His jaw is scruffy, his skin bright red and flushed. Baggy, bloodshot eyes glare at us.

"You can't be here," I say immediately. "You're violating your restraining order."

"Where's my son?" he slurs.

"Not your concern anymore," Law says.

"Yes, it is. He's my kid. I need to speak some sense into him."

Law steps closer, but I try to pull him back. He shakes me off and lowers his voice when he addresses Davis's dad. "He may be your kid, but you don't get to have anything to do with him anymore." He turns to me. "Call the cops."

"My phone's on the bus," I say.

"Get mine at the front of the dojo."

My heavy footsteps pound through the bamboo curtain. I search along the entire front wall but can't see a phone.

"What's going on?" one of my students asks. I don't know which one—I'm too distracted by finding Law's phone to focus.

"Nothing," I say. "But no matter what you hear, you're all to stay in here. Understand?"

Yelling comes from the reception area, and I finally spot Law's phone on the floor, plugged into a charger. My feet stumble over themselves to get to it, and my hands tremble trying to unplug it. I need to get back to Law as soon as possible, but that's not going to happen if I can't unplug this fucking phone.

I end up yanking the thing out.

By the time I rush back to the reception area, Mr. Sullivan's on the floor with Law pinning him down and swinging punches.

Frozen by what I'm seeing, and the phone call to the cops forgotten, I don't realise I'm not moving. I can't. My feet are like lead. "Law, stop!"

At least my mouth works.

He doesn't.

When I see blood spatter from Mr. Sullivan's mouth, my legs finally give in. I rush over to Law and grip his shoulder, but he tries to fight me off—like he doesn't know who's the enemy anymore—so I dig my thumb in hard. "Stop," I say again.

Law breathes heavy, snapping out of whatever trance he's disappeared into. He stares down at a knocked out and bloody Mr. Sullivan and then back at me. "He swung first."

His words aren't defensive but more unsure than anything else. Like he doesn't believe them himself.

I purse my lips, because Law doesn't have a mark on him. Even if it's true, the cops aren't going to believe him. "I have to call an ambulance … and the cops."

His mouth drops open to protest, but he knows he can't. "Okay." Law rolls off Mr. Sullivan and sinks to the floor beside him.

"Is that … Is that my dad?" Davis asks from the doorway. Other students flank him. I should've known better than to tell a group of teenagers *Don't look over there!*

"Get back in the dojo," I order, and something about my rigid voice makes them obey me, no questions asked. I never lose my cool with the kids—not even when they hounded me about my sexuality. I stand guard at the bamboo partition between the reception area and the classroom.

Law and I don't speak as we wait for the cops and ambulance to show up. Mr. Sullivan regains consciousness, mumbles something about faggots, and then closes his eyes again. He hasn't passed out though. He groans and carries on in pain. His face is purple and swelling more by the minute, and blood drips from his presumably broken nose. Yeah, it's bad, but he's acting as if he's dying. There's no doubt in my mind he's going to milk this for everything it's worth.

My fears are confirmed when the police walk in and the first thing Mr. Sullivan says is "I want to press charges."

Fuck.

14

REED

Brief statements are taken when the police arrive, but because of the class of students in the other room—who I inform the cops saw nothing—the officers tell me to go to the station to make a proper statement after the kids are picked up by their parents.

When Mr. Sullivan is taken out on a stretcher, and handcuffs are slapped on Law's wrists, I call out to the students. "Let's go. Back to the bus."

All I want to do is chase after Law and make sure he's okay. Surely they'll see Law was acting in self-defence. Davis's dad has a restraining order against him. Law was protecting his student. I run what happened over in my mind several times. It's highly probable that Mr. Sullivan threw the first punch. He's drunk and a violent person. But with no one there to see it, and the physical damage only on him, Law could be in a lot of trouble.

"Mr. Garvey?" Davis says, and I snap out of my worried trance. "What was my dad doing here?"

The other kids have filed out of the dojo and onto the street. I need to go with them, but I trust them not to do something insanely stupid in the five minutes I need to talk to Davis. "He wanted to see you. We told him he couldn't because of the restraining order. When I came to grab Law's phone, your dad tried to attack him. Law defended himself."

"But why was my dad here? Why did he want to see me?"

"He didn't say. And I'm sorry, but I don't think you should get your hopes up. He was drunk and argumentative. He might've been here to yell at you or … I don't know, try to attack you again."

Davis nods, but it breaks my heart to see the glimmer of hope still shining in his eyes. Maybe his dad was here to make amends, but we all know statistics aren't on his side on that one.

I direct Davis and the kids back to the school bus, and as soon as I get there, I grab my phone out of the driver's side door so I can send a quick text to Brody.

Reed: *Need you at Carindale Police Station. ASAP.*

My phone pings on the way back to the school, but I force myself not to check it while I'm driving. The parents have gathered in a group by the time we make it back to campus. The clock on the bus dashboard says we're twenty minutes late. After waiting for the cops and the ambulance and then giving quick statements, I didn't realise time had slipped away.

Shit.

The kids disperse, no doubt filling the parents in about the day's events. This whole thing is a mess. There'll be reports to fill out, parents given an official statement, and a whole lot more other stuff I'm going to have to deal with, but I just don't have the time now. I'm going to get in trouble for not staying and talking to each parent individually, but there's a more pressing matter, and I don't care about the repercussions.

"Davis, come with me," I say, and we make our way over to his mother.

"This is bad, isn't it?" Davis asks. He avoids looking at the group of parents and students gawking in this direction, but that doesn't mean he can't feel the burn of their stares like I can. "Guess it's my turn to be in the school news this week. How long do you think they'll gossip about this?"

"Don't worry about anything. I'll handle it, okay?"

Mrs. Sullivan is crying before we even get to her. Her eyes are red-rimmed, and I get the feeling she's been crying a lot longer than just now when we pulled up. "What did he do? He turned up at the dojo, didn't he?"

I nod.

She hugs her son and then checks over him. "Did he hurt you?"

"Didn't get a chance. Law got to him first," Davis says.

"He's at the hospital," I add. "Your husband, I mean. Not Law. He was arrested."

Her eyes widen. "What?"

"He tried to attack Law, who's a trained martial arts instructor. You do the math. I'm sure your husband is fine, but he's pressing charges."

Mrs. Sullivan frowns. "But he broke a restraining order. He called today. Says he wants to come home. I told him no."

"I need to get to the police station to find out what's going on. Maybe you two should go to the hospital and find out what he wants, and if he's willing to keep his hands to himself in the future."

"No, we'll come to the police station," she says.

"Mum," Davis complains. "What if he wants to come home because he accepts me?"

His mum's eyes fill with sympathy and disappointment. "Honey …" Her mouth shuts.

"What?" he asks.

I don't need to use my imagination to guess what he said to her on the phone.

"He wants to send you to your grandparents' to live so he can move back in," she whispers.

Yup, that'll do it. I want to reach out to Davis to comfort him, but instead of being upset like I expect, Davis turn red and looks ready to explode.

"Fucking what?" he screeches.

"I told him no. I'm so sorry, hon."

"Uh, you two have a lot to talk about, and I need to get to the police station," I say awkwardly.

"We'll meet you there," Mrs. Sullivan says and wraps her arm around her son.

I drop my bus keys off at the office but don't bother going to my classroom to lock up. There's nothing important kept in there anyway, and I don't have time. As soon as I'm back at my car, I pull out my phone and check my messages.

Brody: *Did someone steal your phone? The Reed I know would never need to use police station and ASAP in the same sentence.*

Reed: *Not for me. Long story. Please?*

Brody: *Already here. Who am I here for exactly?*

Reed: *Law. Full name is Lawson Steele.*

Brody: *I'm not allowed to make a joke here about Law breaking the law, am I?*

Reed: *No. I'll meet you there in fifteen.*

Brody: *On it.*

Even though I've only been there once before, I arrive at the police station on autopilot with no recollection of how I get here. I find Brody at reception, and he pulls me aside.

"What's going on?" I ask.

"They're holding him until they get the complainant's full statement," Brody says.

"So, what can I do to help?"

"I told them I'm Lawson's attorney—"

"Whoa, we can't afford you. I asked you to come as my friend and for some free advice."

He cocks his head and gives his derisive look that hasn't changed since high school. "Pro bono. And don't think for one second that 'we' comment will slide, but we'll come back to that. They'll want to take your formal statement. They showed me the cops' notes, and they say you didn't see what happened."

"I was getting Law's phone when it all went down."

"From what I can gather, they're both claiming the other one is responsible. If this Sullivan guy attacked first, Law can claim self-defence."

I don't look at my friend as I say, "And if Law started the fight?"

"Fight? If he started it, he can be charged for assault

with the aim to cause grievous bodily harm. His victim's in the hospital, for crying out loud."

"Sullivan beat his gay son," I hiss.

Brody flinches but slips back into lawyer mode immediately. "That'll work in Law's favour, and he might get a lenient sentence, but he's a martial arts instructor. He knows how to incapacitate someone without trying to mangle their face. If he's charged with anything, there's a chance they'll push for a harsh sentence. Worst case, he's looking at jail time. Best case, maybe probation, community service … but, uh, you should know that someone with an assault on their record will be stripped of their blue card to work with kids—"

"He can't lose his dojo."

"He should've thought of that before he attacked a parent."

Screw that. Law cannot lose his program or his students. He's the best teacher I know. Hell, he's the best person I know. Even with the lying, he's still better than the majority of most humans. He's kind, funny, passionate, and … fuck, I miss him. I miss being his friend, and I miss having him in my bed. I want him. Need him. Don't want to be without him.

Holy shit.

Well then. I storm over to the desk and the officer who was talking to Brody. "I want to make my official statement. Mr. Sullivan swung at Lawson first. It was self-defence. Mr. Sullivan also has an assault record. We were in here with Sergeant Boyd a few weeks ago with his son, filing for a domestic violence order against him."

The officer looks down at the file in front of him and then back at me. "You're Reed Garvey?"

I nod.

"In the notes the officers took at the scene, you said you didn't see anything. You were getting Lawson Steele's phone and were out of the room."

"I returned just in time to see Mr. Sullivan try to hit Lawson."

The officer sighs as if he doesn't believe me, and then Brody drags me away again back to our corner.

"What the fuck are you doing?" he growls.

"Saving Law's ass. He's not in the wrong here. I have no doubt Sullivan attacked first. Law's dojo is all about order and never using their techniques unless they have to." Although, when I found Law, he wasn't in any type of control. I shake that thought free though. He's not the type of guy to lose it without reason. I don't know him well, but I know at least that much.

"Committing perjury isn't going to help you," Brody whispers.

"Law is innocent."

"You're really strung up over this guy, aren't you?" Brody's tone is mostly inquisitive, but I tell myself to ignore the hurt undertone. Brody and I ... we'd never work.

"Well, yeah. I kinda am," I say truthfully.

He sighs. "Okay then. Let's get him bailed out as fast as we can so you two can sort your shit. But you should tell him if he ever lies to you again, I won't hesitate in kicking his ass, even if he is my client."

I'd like to see him try to kick a martial arts instructor's ass. "You looove me."

"Shut up."

My face falls when I realise I haven't called Law's brother yet. "I should call Anders."

"Real Anders or fake Anders?"

I ignore Brody and take out my phone and call Anders, and then when Law's phone rings in my pocket, I want to kick myself. Of course, I don't have Anders' number. Luckily, Law's phone doesn't have a passcode, and I can use his.

I wait for the anger over the phone thing to build. It's a reminder of what Law did to me, but it doesn't trigger the same feelings of betrayal. Law's more important to me than a petty grudge over something that got blown out of proportion. In hindsight, I'm a dumbass for not knowing something was wrong sooner. I was too busy wrapped up in my crush on Law while sleeping with his brother to realise I already had the thing I wanted the whole time.

I want Law.

15

LAWSON

So, jail isn't fun. Shocking, really. I'm only in a holding cell, so it's not like I run the risk of being someone's bitch when I'm the only one in here, but still, the whole place smells like urine, it's small enough to induce claustrophobia, and the bare walls and no belongings means I have no idea how long I've been in here.

I don't know what came over me in the dojo. The only thing I know for sure is the guy tried to hit me first, and what I did was so far past self-defence I have no idea what'll happen to me now.

I might lose everything, all because I couldn't control myself. That makes me no better than Davis's dad or even Kyle.

Dropping onto the small bench in the cell, I rest my head in my hands.

Kyle. He's still doing time for trying to kill Anders. Yet, when I was punching Mr. Sullivan, I was envisioning him.

The man tried to take my brother away from me, and I didn't realise I haven't dealt with that. Not properly.

The door to my cell swings open, and I jump to my feet.

"You're being released," the officer says.

"On bail?"

He scoffs. "No. All charges are dropped."

My eyebrows soar high, and my chest fills with relief, but I can't help wondering if this is a trick or I'm dreaming or … "What? Why?"

Another man appears in the doorway. His suit looks expensive, his brown hair is messy, and he's super hot. "As your lawyer, I advise you to keep your mouth closed and accept that there won't be any charges. Get out of here before they change their minds."

"I have a lawyer?"

Hot lawyer rolls his eyes. "I'm Brody." When I don't reply, he says, "Brody Wallace."

Still doesn't help me. "Am I supposed to know that name?"

"Ouch," he says. "I'll be having words with Reed about that."

"R-reed?"

"Come talk to him yourself. He's in the waiting area with Davis and his mother."

My feet can't move fast enough. I'm led through halls and a key-coded door, am given my belongings, and told to sign some papers, but when I find Reed, cement enters my shoes and I slow down. I want to ask why he's still here, and why the Sullivans are here, but I don't. I can't make my mouth move no matter how hard I try.

It takes forever for me to reach them even though they're only a few feet away.

"I suggest we don't have a discussion about this in a police station," Brody says. He takes us through the front doors and into the parking lot. The night is sticky with Queensland humidity, and sweat drips down my back while the air tries to stifle me. Or maybe it's the close call with losing my future that's affecting me.

"What the hell happened while I was in there?" I ask.

"Well," Brody says, "Dipshit number one over here"—he points to Reed—"wrote an affidavit swearing he saw Mr. Sullivan swing first."

My brow furrows. "But—"

"And then dipshit number two over there"—he points to Davis—"corroborated Reed's story. *Apparently*, he was in a position where he could see through the bamboo curtains. They lied to protect you." He lowers his voice and mumbles, "For some reason."

"Guys … I …" I have no idea what to say to that.

Davis approaches me and wraps his arms around my waist. I stand awkwardly for a split second before returning the hug. "Thank you. For protecting me."

This is why I do what I do. For moments like this. I don't need a thanks, but the fact he's giving it willingly—that he knows I'll have his back if he ever needs me—it makes all this bullshit worth it.

"This is the second time you've been there for my son. I can't … there are no words," Mrs. Sullivan says.

"We'd do the same for any student," I say.

She gives us a warm smile. "Come on, Davis, let's get

you home and give your teachers a chance to talk. And we can discuss punishment for lying to the police."

Davis groans, but as they walk off, his mother turns and winks at us. I don't think she's really mad at him for saving me, but she probably can't let him get away with no consequences at all.

"I'm heading off too," my lawyer says and turns to me. "I'll send you the bill, right?"

"Uh, umm …" If I thought my heart started beating harder the second I laid eyes on Reed, I was mistaken. It's palpitating now.

"You ass," Reed says to Brody. "He's not charging us. I already made sure of that."

Us. I like the sound of that.

"Ugh, there you go talking in *we* and *us* again," Brody says. "I'm out."

"Hey!" my brother yells from the other end of the parking lot. "What the hell is going on?"

"On second thought," Brody says, eyeing Anders up and down. "I think I might stay right here." He continues to watch my brother as he makes his way over to us.

I don't know what to think about that. Anders looks exactly like me, but Brody seems … indifferent to me. I lean in and mutter to Reed, "Who is this guy?"

"My only friend in this city. He's also kinda my ex, but not, and he's the only person I have right now."

Explains the indifference but also makes my guilt ten times worse. "Reed, I'm so sorry—"

"Don't. You don't need to apologise. I—"

"Seriously, bro," Anders says as he finally reaches us. "You were arrested?"

"It's all fixed now," Brody says. "I'm his lawyer, Brody Wallace." He holds out his hand, and Anders hesitates before shaking it.

Shit, Anders might be on the edge of running away from Brody. There's interest flared in his eyes, but Brody's all wrong. He's tall, built, a pretty boy still, but not eighteen, and definitely not boyish in the physique department. Anders' kryptonite.

"Can someone tell me what's going on?" Anders asks.

"Sure, I'll fill you in," Brody says. "I think Law and Reed have some things to discuss. There's a café up here. Want coffee?"

Anders' eyes almost bug out of his head.

"It's okay," Reed says to my brother. "I can vouch for Brody."

Anders flicks his gaze from me to Reed to Brody and then back to Reed. With another encouraging nod from Reed, Anders gestures for Brody to lead the way.

"I don't know whether to be proud of him or scared for him right now," I say as they disappear up the street.

"Brody's a good guy. At least, he was five years ago when I knew him."

I turn to Reed. "Why did you lie to the cops for me?"

"Because you didn't deserve to be in there after what he did."

"How do you know he tried to hit me first? I don't have a great track record with you when it comes to lying."

Reed steps closer. "I know you wouldn't lie about something so big."

"How can you trust me after—"

"Because I'm in love with you, you idiot."

His words hit me at the same time my heart stops beating. I'm half-convinced I heard him incorrectly.

"What, nothing to say to that?"

"I … umm …" I lean back against the random car I'm next to. "I've had a really long day, and I don't know if this is happening right now or I've fallen asleep in my jail cell and am wishing for it to be true."

Reed smiles and boxes me in, pressing against me. His lips are tentative when they find mine, but then they meld into a slow and perfect kiss. "Is that real enough for you?"

I shake my head.

This time when he moves closer, Reed also grips the back of my neck and pulls my mouth down to meet his demanding lips and strong tongue. He groans. "I've missed this."

I pull back. "Not to be a total dick here or anything, but this is technically our first kiss. All those other times, you thought I was Anders."

"First of all, this is our second kiss. You kissed me as Law that night your nightmares came back. And second of all, you're wrong. So many times I was with Anders, I was thinking about how I wanted it to be you. I wanted you to be gay."

"Will you settle for bi?"

"Absofuckinglutely if it means I get to be with you."

I cup Reed's face as I bring our foreheads together. "I love you too, by the way. I wanted you from the first time you opened your mouth. I didn't know it could be something like this, but I wasn't going to let you get away that night. I hate myself for lying, because if I'd sat at the table and apologised for my brother being unable to make it, we still could've had fun."

"Would you have had the courage to come home with me though?"

"Probably not," I admit.

"Maybe it was supposed to be this way then."

I highly doubt that, but I want to believe it. "Maybe," I murmur.

"We should go back to my place and talk," Reed says.

"Right. Talk."

I push Reed against the glass wall between his living room and bedroom, just like the first night we met.

Reed groans into my mouth when my hips thrust against him, our cocks rubbing and lining up in a needy search for each other.

"Wait." He pulls back. "We were supposed to be talking."

"My cock says I need you, if that counts."

Reed laughs and pushes me off him. "Nice try." He laces his fingers with mine and leads me to his couch.

My heart beats strong against my chest when Reed sits close enough for me to wrap my arm around him.

"I …umm, don't exactly know where we go from here," he says. "I know what I want, but it might be a bit much for you. I … uh—" He swallows hard enough for me to hear the gulp.

"I want everything," I say without hesitation. "I want to

introduce you to Anders properly—as my boyfriend. I want you to meet my parents—hmm, actually, I should probably come out to them first, but that won't be a problem. They were great when Anders came out. A little caught off-guard, but they'll know how to react better this time."

"We don't have to rush this. Just knowing you want something more than … whatever the hell we can call what we were doing before."

"But I want to do this right. I want to meet your sister … although, a trip to Europe probably isn't in the cards. Maybe we could go halves in getting her a plane ticket over here instead. I want to do this for real."

"Why do I sense a *but* coming?"

"Anders still needs me. It's not as bad as it once was, but there will be nights I'll disappear because of him. And—"

"Break up with guys for him?"

"I've told him I'm not doing that for him anymore, but I'm not going to lie—I've told him that repeatedly before and I still do it."

"You don't … hook up with them or anything, right?"

I bark out a laugh. "Fuck no. I flinch away if they even try to hold my hand. Not because they're guys, but because Anders only dates dickheads."

"Thanks."

I grin. "You were different. You were a blind date. The usual guys I break up with for him are guys he's been seeing for a month or so. You're the only guy I've ever …"

"You know you're enabling him—"

"I do know that. I also know it'll piss you off if I choose him over you sometimes."

Reed shakes his head. "No. I get it and I'll understand,

but have you two ever thought of, you know, going to therapy?"

"Anders is in therapy, and after the incident with Sullivan, I realise I need it too. I shouldn't have lost my head the way I did tonight." I stare down at my cracked knuckles and the dried blood on my hands. I haven't even had a chance to wash it off yet, and when we arrived at Reed's apartment, all I could think about was being close to him. Being inside him. Wanting him.

Reed's hand covers mine. "Let's get you cleaned up in the shower. Let someone take care of you for once." His gentle hands pull me up from the couch, and I sway a little. All the fight and adrenaline from the night has left, and I can barely stand.

A few minutes ago, I was ready to maul Reed until neither of us could move anymore.

Instead, with a few small words, Reed's brought me to surrender, and I'm under his complete control. The knowledge that he wants to take care of me in a way that no one ever has ... I fall for him even more.

He undresses me slowly and peppers light kisses along my jaw and neck. Big hands roam my torso, and I'm too exhausted to do anything but let him explore me.

He lathers me up and massages over my tired body, cleaning every inch of me, including my bloodied hands. Once they're clean, he raises my fingers to his mouth, slowly kissing each one.

"You did nothing wrong today," Reed whispers.

"Yes, I did. I lost control."

"You were protecting someone you care about, and when I told you to stop, you stopped." Reed's mouth moves from my hand to my wrist and up my arm. "I know you'd never do anything to hurt me."

"Never." I cup his face and bring my mouth down on his. I turn us so I can push him against the wall of the shower. He grunts and tries to push me off him, but I hold firm.

"I need this," I say.

"I'm still supposed to be taking care of you." Reed overpowers me and spins me so I'm the one against the cold tile.

His lips trail down my chest as he sinks to his knees, and I'm torn. I want to pull him back up and ask him to just hold me, but my cock wants his mouth more. The second his tongue moves over my tip, I reach the point of no return.

"God, I love you," I say and run my thumb over his cheek.

Reed smiles and takes me into his mouth, while my hand moves to his blond hair.

"I didn't think … I thought …" I can't get the words past my lips. I thought this would never happen again. I thought I'd lost Reed for good.

In the past, I've never cared when a relationship has ended. I couldn't handle it when Reed broke up with me, and it was even worse when he found out the truth. I've barely slept. I've been struggling through my classes, one of which resulted in a student making contact with another and almost knocking them out.

I've never felt like this about anyone before. I pull out of his mouth and lift him under his arms.

"What's wrong?" he asks.

"I just … I want … need." I officially can't string sentences together anymore.

Reed laughs. "You've had a long day. How about we get out and go to bed."

I bury my face in his neck and whisper against his skin. "Thank you for forgiving me."

"I would say don't do it again, but we're both going to fuck up at some point."

"I promise never to lie to you again. That's one thing I can do."

"That, and I know when you're lying now, thanks to your brother."

I smirk. "That traitor. You two are going to gang up on me now, aren't you?"

"Count on it. Come on. Bed."

My hands refuse to let him go, though. Towelling off is entertaining when he dries himself off and then just gets wet again when I pull him against me. He catches on quick and dries me first the next time, all the while laughing and trying to nudge me away from him.

"Baby, you need sleep," Reed says.

"I need you. Only you." I push him down on the bed and blanket his body with mine. It's my turn to explore him as I pin him to the mattress.

"Law." It's not his raspy croak that makes me pause.

I pull back and stare into his eyes. "Say it again."

"Your name?"

I nod.

Reed's lips quirk. "You might have to earn it."

My fingers pinch his nipple, and he flinches.

"Whoa, that's not gonna do it." He laughs.

"I hate you."

Reed reaches for his bedside table, and the move forces

me to sit up. "Nope. You love me." He flings a condom at my head, but I manage to catch it. "And you're gonna show me how much."

I tear open the foil packet, but instead of rolling it on me, I put it on him.

His hand grips mine, stilling them. "Are you sure?"

I answer by finishing the job and lubing up his latex-covered dick.

He rises to his knees next to me, pulling me close. "If you're not ready …"

"I chickened out last time, and I think it had nothing to do with you or not being physically ready. It was because I didn't want to do this while deceiving you. I want all of you."

"You want to roll over? It might be easier to … you know …"

I lie on my back. "I want it like this. Face to face."

Reed's hands shake but he hides it by covering my body with his. He lubes his fingers and begins stretching me. The nerve endings send a jolt of pleasure to my balls and cut off my oxygen supply. With my stilted breathing, Reed hesitates, but I whisper my encouragement in forms of "more" and "keep going."

There's a pinch when the third one enters me, but I crave the burning. My legs tremble as he rubs over my prostate again and again, and my dick goes impossibly hard.

"Reed …" I don't need to finish my sentence.

His fingers are replaced with his cock, and he eases himself inside. I breathe hard, and Reed gives me a chance to adjust. The last thing I see before I slam my eyes shut to ride out the sting is Reed's assessing face, and I cut him off before he can ask if I'm sure. "Just need a sec."

"Here," he says, his hands going to my knees and pushing them up, so I'm nearly bent in half. His cock slides in even deeper and reaches that spot inside me that makes me want to explode.

When he moves inside me, I get to that euphoric state where I want it to last forever but end at the same time. He goes slow, torturing me. When he grips my cock with his strong hand, my spine tingles in a way that lets me know I don't have long left.

A sheen of sweat breaks out over my body, and my stomach muscles contract, and when Reed tells me to come, my body goes off on its own accord, as if it was waiting for his permission.

Ropes of cum hit my stomach and chest, and I'm too lost in the pleasure of it to even feel Reed in my ass as he picks up his pace. When he finally stills inside me, I come back to the present and am keenly aware of the cramp in my leg and the pain in my ass, but all of it fails to make an impact on the way Reed lights up my Goddamn world when I stare up at his satisfied grin.

16
REED

After we clean up, Law curls into my side, and I let out a content sigh. "This is weird," I say.

"Weird how?"

"You're not running off on me."

Law buries his head into my neck. "I'm not pretending to be someone I'm not."

"Are you saying you wouldn't have run off all those times if I knew it was you?"

"When …" He hesitates and then tries again. "When I was with you as Anders, I tried not to even talk. I was sure I'd fuck it up by saying something I said as Law or—"

I laugh when I think about it. "You did that a few times, but I never picked up on it. Like the way you call me teach. I thought it was a case of sharing similar mannerisms and vocabulary as your brother, which would make sense because you live together."

"Not everything was untrue. I really am as tone deaf as a fish."

"I still maintain you can't know if fish are tone deaf."

"I didn't want to lose you, and I didn't know how the truth could come out without that happening."

"I am interested to know how long you would've kept it up."

"Probably not much longer. Anders knew something was going on. We were on our way to dinner for me to confess everything to him when you stormed in and kinda did it for me."

"Oh."

"And I didn't know how long I could stand ignoring you when you thought I was pissed over the Anders thing instead of the truth, which is you rejected me."

I poke Law in the ribs. "I didn't know it was you I was rejecting."

He sighs. "I'm sorry I fucked us up."

"We're here now." I kiss the side of his head.

Sleep tries to pull me under, and Law's breathing evens out, but before I can drift off, a vibrating noise fills the quiet space. I figure it's one of our phones, and when it stops a minute later, I close my eyes again. But the vibrating comes back.

Slipping out of bed carefully so I don't wake Law, I find the culprit in the form of Law's phone and Anders' name blinking at me.

"Hello?" I whisper into the phone.

"Law?" Anders voice sounds strained. "I fucked up. I'm fucked up." He breathes hard.

"Anders," I say louder. "It's Reed. Law's asleep."

"Shit. Umm. Never mind. Don't tell him I called."

Before I can get him to tell me what's wrong, he disconnects the call.

So, it starts already. What am I supposed to do here? Law's had a long night and needs his rest, but I don't like the way Anders sounded. Law only told me hours ago that Anders will always be his first priority, but if Anders doesn't want him knowing …

No, there's definitely something wrong.

"Law." I shake him, and he grumbles but doesn't wake. "Lawson. It's Anders."

He bolts upwards. "What's wrong?"

"I don't know. He told me not to tell you, but he said he fucked up and then realised he was talking to me and not you, so he hung up."

Law slumps down in bed and lets out a loud breath. "Okay, I'm up." His eyes stay closed.

I snort. "Looks it."

With a groan, he climbs out of bed and rummages for his clothes.

"Want me to come with you?"

He hesitates.

"If you think it'll be better to go alone, that's okay. You can borrow my car."

"Shit. I forgot mine's at home. And no, I want you there. I don't know what's going on, but if he's freaking out, it might be a good idea for you to see why I need to disappear sometimes. Anders won't like it, but he can do this one thing for me. I don't want you to resent me for picking him all the time."

"I won't ever do that."

Law crosses the room and brushes his lips against mine. "We need to go."

I throw on whatever clothes I can find and follow Law into the parking garage under my building. "Did you want to drive? I don't know where you guys live." The one time I dropped him home, he told me to pull over on the busy street and he jumped out fast so I didn't hold up traffic. All I know is it's close enough to the dojo for Law to walk to and from work.

"Yeah, I kinda did that on purpose." He holds out his hand, and I throw him my keys.

Law's silent on the drive, but when we turn onto the street of the dojo, he pulls into a four-storey apartment block. "If we can find a visitor's spot in the carpark it should be okay. Otherwise we'll need to find street parking which is a bitch."

After he finds a spot okay, and we walk up three flights of stairs, Law stops outside apartment 3B and turns to me.

He's antsy and wrings his hands. His eyes have that worried look shining right at me. "Depending on what state he's in, this might get ugly."

"I can handle it."

Leaning in, he kisses me softly. "Thank you for wanting to be here, but if it's too much, I understand."

I stop his hand from reaching for the doorhandle. "Don't you get it? Now we're doing this, your issues are my issues. I'm not going anywhere, even if he's in there naked, wielding a knife and promising his life to Satan."

The door swings open and Anders stands there, his eyes red-rimmed and with a scowl on his face. "Satan doesn't love me. He's only using me for sex."

"What's going on?" Law asks.

Anders' gaze turns to me. "You ratted me out?"

"Your phone call was—"

Anders steps aside to let us in the apartment. "I'm fine. I just—"

The loudspeaker in their living room belts out "Detroit Rock City."

"KISS?" Law asks. "You're so not fine."

"I realised something," Anders says, "and then I called because I didn't know what time it was, and I told your boyfriend not to say anything, and then—"

"Yeah, because saying 'I'm fucked' and then hanging up isn't going to raise some flags," I say.

"Your friend. Cody, Bodhi … whatever his name was—"

"Brody. And I'm so telling him you forgot his name. His ego won't like that."

"Yeah, him. He filled me in about the kid and what you two did for him a few weeks back."

"That fucker," Law mumbles.

"No," Anders says. "I needed it. I needed to hear what you kept from me, because I know exactly why you did it. It made me realise how much I've put on you, Law. It ends. Tonight. I'm done leaning on you and needing you, and I'm going to do better."

"And how's that going for you?" Law gestures to the speakers where the music is playing.

"I'm freaking out, obviously. But I'm going to do it. I called to tell you until Reed informed me it was the middle of the night. I lost track of time."

"Are you sure that's all it was?" Law asks.

Anders swallows hard as he looks away. "Yup."

Law sighs. "Okay, you're lying, but we'll be in my room if you need us. I'm wrecked." He grabs my hand and leads me to his bedroom, closing the door behind us. "Mmm, bed." He flops down on his mattress in his otherwise barren room.

"Who decorated in here?" Even my apartment has more flair, and I've only just moved in. I'm almost curious to sneak across the apartment into Anders' room. If I had to guess, I'd say it'd be cluttered with crap. Law said they try to be polar opposites when it comes to personal choices.

"Mmmhglerh."

With a laugh, I strip down to my underwear and climb into bed next to a fully dressed Law. "Go to sleep, baby."

He's already out of it.

Anders' pacing sends tremors through the small apartment with each heavy footstep, and I wonder if I should go out there and check on him, but it's not my place. I'm also reluctant to leave Law. Now that I have him, I don't want to be away from him, even for a moment. A little voice inside my head that sounds a hell of a lot like my ex's rings through my head warning me not to be clingy, but there's a difference between wanting to be with someone always and *needing* to be with someone.

I need Law in my life, there's no doubt about that, but that doesn't mean I have to live in his pocket. I just want to.

I stare at his unfairly good looks, his relaxed face, and slightly parted lips, and I know without a doubt I'm so far gone for this guy I'll do anything to make him happy.

It takes a while for me to fall asleep because I have the

irrational fear that when I wake up, he'll be gone. At some point during the night, I wake to an empty bed, but hearing Law's and Anders' voices travel through the walls lulls me back into sleep. When I wake again, there's some random guy next to me, staring at me with a wide smile.

"What the fuck?" I flinch back and scramble out of bed.

The guy laughs. "What, you don't recognise your own boyfriend?"

My heart rate calms but not enough. I grab my chest. "Your beard. It's …"

"Anders made me shave it to prove he's going to do better. Is it really that bad?" Law rubs over his jaw and chin.

I mockingly assess him. Without his beard, Law's even hotter than before. His jaw is predominantly square, which is only emphasised by his naked skin. "Might have to see if your brother is still available," I joke.

"It'll grow back."

I grin. "You still look hot."

Law reaches for me and pulls me down on top of him. His smooth skin moves against the stubble on my own face.

"Feels weird," I whisper. "I got used to the beard."

"Well, now you can get used to the smoothness." When Law kisses me, I can't hold back my groan.

"No more beard rash," I say.

"No more lying."

"No more handling everything on your own."

Law smiles. "Here's one for you, no more committing perjury to save my ass."

"How about no more getting arrested?"

"That'll work too. But seriously, if anyone found out you lied to the cops for me …"

"I'd do it again in a heartbeat. You mean the world to me, and I'll do anything to protect you. Some lies are worth the end result."

"Love you," he whispers.

"Love you too."

17

LAWSON

SIX MONTHS LATER

"Our little boy's all grown up." I wipe away a fake tear.

Reed smiles. "He hasn't gone through with it yet, and by the look of him, he might faint. Or throw up."

We stare at Anders from the other side of the restaurant while he tries to break up with his recent guy. The sweat on his brow is visible from here. I want to sit back and let him do this on his own, but my protective instincts urge me to go over there and save him.

It's the first time he's been with someone since I shaved my beard. Without his safety net, Anders hasn't been game enough to date, but he's getting there. And if he can do this, then Reed and I can break our news to him.

Reed reaches for my hand across the table. "If he can't do it, it's not a big deal. We'll wait."

"We need to tell him soon," I say. "Our lease begins in a week." In a *house*, not an apartment. I haven't had a backyard since I was a kid, and I'm kinda excited about it. Embarrassingly so.

"So, I move all my stuff in and wait for you," Reed says.

I grab the water in front of me and take a sip to wet my dry mouth. "Maybe I can sneak my furniture out and then just not tell him I moved out."

"And do you plan on paying twice the rent forever, Mr. Money Bags? I mean, my inheritance is still there if we need it, but—"

"We're not touching that money," I say. He confessed to me once when I accidently saw his bank statement that he's saving that money for when he goes to have kids. It's something he's always wanted. It came as no surprise after the way he is with his students. He'll make a great dad one day.

I hope to be the guy who goes on that journey with him, but it's only been six months. An awesome six months, sure, but still way too premature to think about kids seriously. I'm still thinking about what dates I can take him on next week, next month, next year. I still have to meet his sister.

This is by far the easiest and best relationship I've ever had, and the first time where I've actually looked forward to a possible future. I don't care what that future is, so long as Reed's in it.

"Maybe we need to rip it off like a Band-Aid," I say, glancing back at my brother.

"That might not be the best idea."

"Do you think it's too soon?" I ask.

"When it comes to Anders, I think it's overdue," Reed

says. "You guys are extremely co-dependent. But that's the issue. Are *you guys* ready? Doesn't matter if it *should* be done, you both need to be comfortable with it."

"I'm so ready to live with you." More than ready.

"Not what I'm asking," Reed says.

"I know," I whisper. I've been protecting my brother for so long now, it seems wrong to be leaving him. Reed thinks it's a twin thing. I think it's that a tragic event occurred, and instead of dealing with it, we both buried our heads in the same sandbox. But we're both getting help, and we need to take this next step. It's hard to admit that it's terrifying, but at the same time, I look at Reed and can't wait to do it.

Reed's been more than patient with us, and it doesn't feel like I'm choosing between him and my brother. I'm choosing to spend my life with Reed. Anders is just going to have to deal with it.

If he can.

Shit. It doesn't take much for the doubt to creep back in.

"We'll see how he handles this and go from there." Reed tips his head in Anders' direction. "I know you're dying to step in there and finish this for him."

"That's because I already know how it's going to end," I say.

"How?"

"I've broken up with *a lot* of guys for Anders, and it nearly always goes the same."

"Which is?"

"This one's got drama written all over him. Actually, nearly all his dates do. But I'm going to go with high-pitched hissy fit tonight. He doesn't look like the type to throw stuff."

"I dunno," Reed says. "I think he'll take it easily. Young guys like him aren't looking for anything serious anyway."

I want to say this guy's only three years younger than Reed, but I don't. I also want to tell him my theory about the young pretty ones having big egos that don't like to be crushed. "Okay, newbie. What's the wager? I predict we have about a minute to settle the terms."

Reed's lips quirk. "Whoever loses bottoms tonight?"

"How is that losing?"

Reed laughs. "Good point. Okay. Loser has to unpack all the moving boxes on their own."

"And break up before we even live together for a whole day? You totally suck at making bets." I lean forward and rest my elbows on the table in front of me. "Loser has to be the one to tell Anders I'm moving out."

Reed clicks his tongue as he thinks about it. "Deal. Now, if you'll excuse me, I have to go to the bathroom."

"But you're about to miss the important part. He's going to do it any second now."

"I'll be super quick."

But my boyfriend is a liar. Instead of heading towards the bathrooms, he interrupts Anders and his date. Reed's hand goes to Anders' shoulder, he says something I can't hear, and then the other guy's mouth drops open, he immediately stands, tips his head in Anders' direction, and walks out the front of the restaurant.

Anders stands and hugs Reed, blowing out a loud breath I can practically hear across the room.

I glare at Reed as they make their way to our table and take their seats. "That was cheating. And you've just fallen into the hole of helping Anders break up with people. Also, how the hell did you get that guy to walk away so easily?"

"Law, what is the one thing eighteen-year-olds don't want?" Reed asks.

"Responsibility," I say.

"He congratulated me on my wife being pregnant." Anders laughs.

"You didn't," I say.

"Oh, I did," Reed says. "Dude was too stunned to be pissed. Ran right out of here."

"That totally could've backfired," I say. "He could've been looking for a closeted married guy to call whenever he got bored."

"Was worth the risk. Besides, most people with even a smidgen of morals don't like it when kids are involved."

"You clearly haven't seen the morally corrupt people Anders usually goes for."

"Dick," Anders says and gives me the finger.

Reed takes a swig of his beer. "Ready to do this? Seeing as I won, the floor's all yours."

"Guess I have to man up or whatever." I slowly turn to my brother but flake out. "What's with that saying anyway? Man up. Like how is doing something you need courage for a manly act?"

"Lawson," Reed says. "Stop stalling."

"Okay." I take a deep breath. "So … umm … we have something we need to tell you."

"You and Reed are moving in together," Anders says for me.

"You know?" I ask.

"Figured. Saw you looking at real estate on your phone

and knew it was only a matter of time. And you've both been super nice lately—"

"Hey, I'm always nice," Reed argues.

"True," Anders says. "But that doesn't mean I don't know you guys were hiding something. I'm happy for you both." His tone is casual, his posture relaxed, but Anders is good at putting on a show. Sometimes when he's had a panic attack in the past, I never saw it coming, because he's good at hiding the small signs.

"Are … are you sure?" I ask.

"I'm a big boy, little brother. I can deal with this. *It's time* for me to deal with this."

I want to believe him, but the truth is, if Reed hadn't stepped in tonight, I don't think Anders would've gone through with the breakup. I know I need to stop helping him just as much as he needs to stop asking, but this is a big change. I don't want him to have a setback because I move out and disrupt what little peace Anders has in his life.

He stares at me with a steely gaze. "I. Can. Do. This. You need to not worry about me anymore. It's not your job. You have a boyfriend and a life. So, go live it."

"The house is only fifteen minutes away from your apartment. I'll still be there if you need me," I say.

"Haven't needed you in the last six months."

This is true. He hasn't until tonight. But he's also in intense therapy twice a week, and if his date tonight is anything to go by, he's not making any progress.

"Seriously, I'll be fine," Anders says. "But now that"—he waves his hand in the direction of the table he was sitting at—"is all over with, I'm going home to shower. I don't think

I've sweated this much since my week-long sex marathon with—"

"We don't need to know. Thanks," I say. My brother, the over-sharer.

"When do you move?" Anders asks as he stands.

"Next week."

He scoffs. "Thanks for the heads-up, dickhead. Now I'm going to have to find a roommate or break the lease. I can't afford that apartment on my own."

"I'll pay my share for a full month. You have time to figure something out."

Anders runs a hand through his hair. "Okay. I'll see you guys at home."

As I stare at Anders' retreating back, Reed moves seats so he's next to me instead of opposite. "You look like you need a drink," he says.

"He took it better than I expected, which makes me worry."

"It's not like we're moving to the other side of the country."

"I know."

Reed hesitates. "Are you sure … are you sure Anders is the only thing you're worried about?"

My brow furrows. "What else would there be?"

"That it's fast. Six months isn't long …"

I reach for his hand. "We practically live together as it is." I might complain every time Reed tries to go home to his apartment. "I've been in relationships in the past that have been nothing but work trying to keep a hold of it. You and I might've had a shitty start, but now … I can't remember what my life was like without you."

"I remember mine. Depressing as fuck. Work, gym, TV. Bam, that was my life."

"Aww, now the only difference is you have me and Anders annoying you."

Reed grins. "Anders isn't as annoying as you are."

"Yet, you still love me."

"For some reason," he murmurs. "I bet it's the black belt thing. You seem badass, but really, you're a big softy."

I cock my eyebrow. "Excuse me. There is nothing *soft* about me, and if we weren't in a crowded restaurant, I'd prove that to you." Under the table, I bring his hand to my crotch.

Reed laughs. "If we weren't meeting up with Brody, I'd let you. But he'll be here any minute."

Ugh. That guy still doesn't like me, but just like I don't want anyone coming in between Anders and me, it's not right for me to get between Reed and Brody. So I try to stay out of it. They're the closest thing each other has to a brother, even though they used to date. I try to keep my jealousy over that fact quiet, but sometimes it slips out. Like right now.

"Are you sure he's not just waiting around for me to fuck up so he can swoop in to get you back?"

"Hell no. Brody and I aren't like that anymore. Never will be. You know that."

I'm not convinced, but I believe Reed when he says he doesn't see Brody that way. I also don't think Brody would go after Reed when he's with me. He's more the type of guy to hang back and wait for the most opportune time to strike.

"Besides," Reed says, "he's been chasing someone else."

My ears perk up. "Really? Who?"

"Won't tell me much, but all he says is he keeps rebuffing him. When he told me that, I immediately liked the guy."

"Then I hope he gets here soon, because I'm starving."

Reed checks the time on his phone. "He should've been here by now. Maybe he got held up at work." Just as he says the words, a text comes through. "Ah, yup. He did. He's not coming. Let's get our food to go."

I lean in and whisper, "Or we could forget dinner completely." The night we met, that sentence was all it took for Reed to proposition me.

Reed's eyes fill with heat as I'm sure he relives the same memory. "There's only one problem with that."

"What's that?" I ask, my voice thick.

"We're at the part of the relationship where food is more important than sex, and you just said you were starving."

As if on cue, my stomach rumbles. "God, we're like an old married couple already."

"I'm totally okay with that."

"Me too."

For the first time in my life, everything is falling into place. Reed's teaching is going better now the students know he's a permanent fixture in the school. His union is gaining more kids every day thanks to Chantel and Davis pointing out it should be open to allies as well. Reed's doing a great job at turning it into so much more than support for the LGBTQ students. It's doing what I hoped to achieve with my martial arts classes. Reduce bullying and promote self-confidence. My dojo's classes are steady, and while Reed and I will never be rich, we love what we do, and we have each other.

That's all we need.

I've found the person who I can not only tolerate for long periods of time, but if he went for it, I'd have no qualms spouting shit about our future and forever, because Reed turned me into a believer.

He's the one.

THANK YOU FOR READING UNWRITTEN LAW!

For any Australians struggling with LGBTI issues, contact one of the following organisations:

QLife. CALL 1800 184 527 or visit qlife.org.au

Lifeline. CALL 13 11 14 or visit https://www.lifeline.org.au/

WHERE TO FIND EDEN FINLEY

www.edenfinley.com

www.facebook.com/EdenFinleyAuthor

Join her Facebook group to receive exclusive snippets, advanced news on releases, and to find ARC opportunities. https://www.facebook.com/groups/1901150070202571/

Eden Finley is an Amazon bestselling author who writes steamy contemporary romances that are full of snark and light-hearted fluff.

She doesn't take anything too seriously and lives to create an escape from real life for her readers. The ideas always begin with a wackadoodle premise, and she does her best to turn them into romances with heart.

BOOKS BY EDEN FINLEY

FAKE BOYFRIEND SERIES
Fake Out (M/M)
Trick Play (M/M)

STEELE BROTHERS
Unwritten Law (M/M)

ROYAL OBLIGATION
Unprincely (M/M/F)

ONE NIGHT SERIES
One Night with Hemsworth (M/F)
One Night with Calvin (M/F)
One Night with Fate (M/F)
One Night with Rhodes (M/M)
One Night with Him (M/F)

ACKNOWLEDGMENTS

I want to thank all of my betas for reading the rough … ROUGH draft. I apologise for my comma deficiency and seriously lacking grammar skills.
Thanks to Kelly from Xterraweb editing for fixing those issues.
To Lori Parks for one last read through to catch ninja typos —they come out of nowhere.
Leslie Copeland, for **everything!**
And to AngstyG for brining Law and Reed to life and making my cover drool-worthy.
Lastly, a big thanks to Linda from Foreword PR & Marketing for helping get this book out into the world.

Printed in Great Britain
by Amazon